"Your Prince has come, *cara*," he drawled sardonically. **"And he intends to marry you."**

Marry her? With a shotgun held to his head? "No!"

"Oh, yes," he said, and even though it was silky soft, there was no mistaking the undercurrent of steely purpose. "My baby will not be born illegitimately—he or she will inherit all that is their due, but that can only be achieved within wedlock."

"Guido—"

"Don't even think of fighting me on this one, Lucy," he said harshly. "I will win."

She looked into his eyes and knew that he meant it. Which meant Lucy Maguire was going to marry a prince.

It should have been a dream come true— but the reality was something different. It meant being shac...

blooded aristocra...

her.

No, it was not a d...

It was a living nightmare.

D0774031

Harlequin Presents®

Introduces a brand-new trilogy by
SHARON KENDRICK

THE
ROYAL HOUSE
OF
CACCIATORE

Passion, power & privilege—the dynasty
continues with these three handsome Princes…

Welcome to Mardivino—a beautiful and wealthy
Mediterranean island principality, with a
prestigious and glamorous Royal family.
There are three Cacciatore princes—
Nicolo, Guido and the eldest, the heir, Gianferro.

Nicolo's story:
The Mediterranean Prince's Passion
#2466

Guido's story:
The Prince's Love-Child
#2472

Gianferro's story:
The Future King's Bride
#2478

Available only from Harlequin Presents®

Sharon Kendrick

THE PRINCE'S LOVE-CHILD

THE ROYAL HOUSE OF CACCIATORE

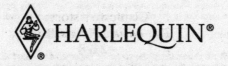

HARLEQUIN®

TORONTO • NEW YORK • LONDON
AMSTERDAM • PARIS • SYDNEY • HAMBURG
STOCKHOLM • ATHENS • TOKYO • MILAN • MADRID
PRAGUE • WARSAW • BUDAPEST • AUCKLAND

With thanks for such wonderful help to:
Neale Hunt—Advertising Maestro.
Paul McLaughlin—Editor of Kroll Inc.'s Report on Fraud.
The Prince of Spin—Olly Wicken.
And to Guy Black, who is a never-ending source of inspiration!

ISBN 0-373-12472-4

THE PRINCE'S LOVE-CHILD

First North American Publication 2005.

Copyright © 2004 by Sharon Kendrick.

www.eHarlequin.com

Printed in U.S.A.

CHAPTER ONE

GUIDO glanced at his watch and a flicker of displeasure briefly spoiled the sensual perfection of his lips.

She was late!

But his irritation gave way to a soft smile as he anticipated the heady delights to come. Lucy could not be blamed for the lateness of her plane—indeed, she did not even know he was going to be there.

Guido found himself wondering what her reaction would be when she discovered that he was, for she was that rare species among women—someone who constantly surprised him.

His eyes flickered to the arrivals board. The plane had landed and soon the flight attendants would be making their way through to the lounge…

Guido was aware of being watched, and his brilliant eyes widened slightly as he saw a woman looking as if she would like to leap on him and devour him. Predictability was so tedious, he decided, turning his head to see the faintest flash of red-brown as a woman with glorious Titian hair sashayed towards the gate. Most of it was hidden beneath a chic little hat, worn at a jaunty angle, but the colour was enough to mark her out, as was the unconscious grace with which she moved.

She was dressed in a sleek navy uniform, her long legs encased in pale silk that he knew would be stockings, not pantyhose. Was it stockings which made a woman walk differently? Guido wondered. Did the feel of cool air on her thighs make her aware of her sexuality? Or was that just something inherent in Lucy's nature?

No. She was a contrast—a maddening and exciting contrast of looks and attitude. Her hair was lit with fire, but her expression was cool, and she seemed oblivious to the men who stood to let her pass and then just carried on standing there, following the sexy sway of her hips with hungry eyes.

He felt the leaping of desire tensing his body but he didn't move. She couldn't yet see him, and he wanted to watch her reaction when she did…

Ahead of her, Lucy could see the jostle of crowds, and the air-conditioning was as cool as ice-water on her skin as she walked through the busy airport. This city held all kinds of associations for her—some good, and some just dangerously good. Hello, New York, she thought.

'Are you coming straight back to the hotel?' Kitty asked.

Lucy turned. Her fellow stewardess was applying a coat of lipstick without the use of a mirror, and Lucy made a silent gesture to indicate that she had smudged it. 'Yes. Why wouldn't I be?'

'Well, I wasn't sure…' Kitty gave a mischievous

grin as she wiped away the errant trace of pink gloss. 'Whether or not you'd be seeing your *Prince*.'

This emphasis on the word was commonplace, and Lucy had grown used to the teasing by now, even though at first she hadn't quite known how to react. It had been a peculiar situation—not just for the rest of the cabin crew, but for her, too. Ordinary girls didn't date princes! And yet it seemed that they did. In fact, they—

But her thoughts were frozen and her steps very nearly followed. Some governing sense of instinct kept her moving forward, forward...because for a minute there she had almost thought she'd seen Guido.

'Isn't that him?' asked Kitty curiously, following the direction of Lucy's stare.

Thank God they were far enough away for him not to be able to see that her face had grown pale. Or at least Lucy was imagining that it *had* grown pale—for surely there would have to be some physical manifestation of the dizzy sensation she was experiencing. As if all the blood had left her veins, leaving her limbs dry and ready to crumple. Keep walking, she told herself. Just keep walking.

'It *is*!' breathed Kitty. 'Oh, my God—it's *him*! He's come to meet you! How romantic is *that*?'

Lucy let her brows slide up beneath the russet curtain of her fringe. 'I don't hear you sounding so surprised when other people's boyfriends come to meet them,' she observed drily.

'That's because other people don't go out with princes,' chided Kitty.

Lucy shook her head. 'He's just a man,' she contradicted faintly, but she knew that her words lacked conviction.

Because he wasn't.

She let her gaze drift over him as she walked towards the brilliant black eyes which had her spotlighted in their sight. Prince or no prince, he was the kind of man most women didn't happen across—not even once in a lifetime.

There was something about the way he carried himself which drew the eye, something about an air of arrogant assurance coupled with a lazy kind of supremacy. Had royal blood and upbringing given him those qualities which seemed to make him stand head and shoulders above the crowd, or would he have had them anyway?

He was standing beside a pillar, half in the shadows, for she knew that he would have sought shelter from prying eyes. Guido had rejected princely life, but its legacy meant that he could never quite shake it off. People were fascinated by the title, but more usually they were fascinated by him—and who could blame them?

Over and over again Lucy had watched as they fawned over him and hung on his every word—men *and* women, but especially women. They drank in the dark, imposing looks, and the sexy, accented drawl, and the careless sensuality which came as naturally to him as breathing.

He was a man in a million—and Lucy still wasn't quite sure what he saw in her. Sometimes she felt as though she was living in a bubble, and that one of these days it was going to burst and she would be left with the dull and rather stark reality of life without Guido.

Don't make it into more than it is, she reminded herself savagely. A casual love affair—nothing more and nothing less. And if, by nature of who he is, he provides a fairytale aspect to the affair—then just enjoy it and don't build it up.

Her half-smile staying in place as though it had been painted on, she waved a quick goodbye to Kitty and walked over to where he waited, a dark and brooding image in cool, expensive linen. The ecstatic clamour of her heart was deafening her, but she gave him a look as steady as any she would give to one of her passengers in First Class who was asking for a glass of champagne.

'Hello, Guido,' she said, in a low, clear voice. 'I wasn't expecting to see you here.'

He might have felt admiration if he hadn't been overwhelmed by frustration. Did nothing affect her bar sex itself? For it was then—and only then—that she let go completely. Looking at the serene smile which seemed to make a mockery of her schoolgirl freckles, he found it hard to imagine her whispering his name, or screaming it, or shuddering with helpless, racking moans against his shoulder.

Guido felt the quickening of his heart, knowing that

his instincts were fighting a battle with his reason. Had it not been her ice-coolness which had set her apart and made him determined to possess her? Had he somehow imagined that he would melt it away completely, leaving her in his thrall—like all the others—so that he could happily walk away?

'Perhaps I would not have bothered if I had known you would give me such a lukewarm welcome,' he parried silkily.

She saw the glitter from his black eyes—recognising now, as she had recognised from the very start, that here was a man who was used to lavish displays of affection and would be bored by them. So she had not given them. From an early age Lucy had learnt to do what people wanted—some might call it people-pleasing; she would define it as making sure she got on with folks.

'So, what would you like me to do?' she murmured. 'Fling my arms around your neck and scream with delight?'

'You can save that for later. In bed,' he returned mockingly, and was rewarded with a faint flush of colour which crept over her pale, freckle-splattered skin.

A blush might be beyond her control, but the flashing light of challenge which sparked from her eyes was not. She lifted her chin and mocked him back. 'Maybe I'm tired and need my sleep.'

'And maybe you don't.' He lifted his hand to her face and slowly drifted a fingertip down over her flushed face, finishing with a deliberately erotic tracing of her lips, which made them tremble slightly and open. He wanted to bend his head to kiss them, but of course he didn't.

He could just imagine the headlines. An erotic and public kiss in newspaper-speak meant only one thing—impending wedding bells.

But if he was cool, then Lucy was cooler still— and his eyes glittered as their gazes mingled.

'Give me your bag,' he said steadily. 'I have the car waiting.'

She had played her part. The necessary part. Not thrown herself into his arms. Hardly even a shiver of pleasure when he had touched her—but enough was enough and Lucy wanted him. Badly. She let him take her small case and allowed herself the luxury of a smile.

'Lovely. Are you driving?'

Lovely? Suddenly he was filled with the need to shatter her icy composure. 'No,' he said softly, as they made their way through the hall, oblivious to the curious glances they attracted. 'I have a chauffeur hidden behind dark glass, so he will be unable to see when I begin to kiss you. The glass is soundproof, too—so that when your breathing begins to quicken as I put my hand up your skirt he will not hear it.'

Her mouth had dried unbearably. 'Oh, Guido, don't,' she whispered.

He felt the exquisite hardness and knew that he must stop this. But not quite yet.

'Nor will he notice when I slide your panties down and pull you onto my lap...'

'Guido—'

'*Hard* down onto my lap.'

'G-Guido—'

He moved his lips to her ear, speaking in a silken whisper as he inhaled her fragrance. 'And I will move you up and down, up and down—filling you completely, until you gasp—'

'Guido!' She was gasping now, her head light, her pulse-rate frantic.

He saw the way her steps had begun to falter, and he caught her by the arm just as a black limousine purred to a halt beside them. In French, he bit out some terse instructions to the driver, and then he propelled her onto the back seat, sliding in beside her and slamming the door shut behind them, imprisoning them in a luxurious, dimly-lit world of their own as he imprisoned her in the warm circle of his arms.

She was so hot with wanting that she could barely speak his name as he pushed her down onto the seat and her hat fell from her head. 'Guido—'

But there was no reply other than the sweet pressure of his mouth as he began to kiss her, transporting her to that place where nothing mattered other than the feel and taste and smell and touch of him. She threaded her fingers luxuriously in the rich ebony satin of his hair and moved her body restlessly against his. And froze in excited horror as she felt his hand on her knee and remembered his words.

Surely he didn't mean to—?

But he was moving his hand, and she was writhing

in response to the direction it was taking, her hips belying the words which she forced herself to say.

'No, we can't,' she protested, her voice slurred with wanting. 'We mustn't. Not here.'

'Why not? The thought of it turned you on. You know it did.' He touched her above the stocking-top, where the bare flesh was a tantalising contrast of cool silk with warm blood pulsing beneath. 'I could read it in your eyes.'

'It may… Oh, God…' Her eyes closed and her head fell back against the soft leather upholstery as his fingertips skated tantalisingly close to where heat seared at her so frustratingly. 'It…it may have turned me on. It doesn't mean it's right.'

The hand stilled. 'Shall I stop, then, *cara mia*?'

Frustration ripped through her. She shook her head helplessly.

He put his lips right up to her ear. He loved her like this. Compliant. His. Her coolness exploding into hot and urgent need. 'I can't hear you, Lucy.'

'No,' she whispered. 'Don't stop. Please don't stop.'

Triumph coursed through him and possessively he pushed aside the panel of her panties to feel the acutely sensitised flesh. But it was over almost before he had started. He could feel her body begin to tense as he pressed his fingertip against her, and she caught him by the neck and dragged his mouth back down on hers, just as her legs splayed and she made soft, moaning noises of pleasure, like a cat.

They stayed like that for a while, their mouths

glued together, his finger still touching her intimately while she continued to spasm against him. When it was over, she drew away, her face sweat-sheened, still shuddering as she shook her head.

'What did you do that for?' She gulped breath into her lungs like a drowning woman.

He smiled as he tugged her uniform skirt back down. 'Because you wanted me to.'

'We should have waited.'

'But you didn't want to.'

No, she hadn't. It had been a long time—too long—and she had missed him. Had he missed her? she wondered. Even a tiny bit? She turned her eyes up to his, but as usual their glittering ebony depths were impenetrable. She wanted to kiss him again, but kissing seemed almost too intimate. How crazy was that after what had just happened?

'And what about you?' she questioned huskily, cupping him quite suddenly. She saw him briefly close his eyes and groan, before snatching her hand away to hold it close to his mouth, letting his breathing grow steady before he spoke.

She could feel his warm breath on her fingertips.

'But I can…wait, *cara*,' he said huskily. 'That is the difference between us.'

He was always so controlled—always—and in demonstrating his own self-discipline he had drawn attention to her own lack of it! But Lucy knew that there was more than his steely resolve at stake here. Physically, she might be able to change his mind, but mentally she didn't stand a chance.

He might have shrugged off all the trappings which came with being a prince, but he never ignored the responsibility which came with the title. His mind would have raced and overtaken the demands of his body. He would have imagined all the worst-case scenarios—them being disturbed by the driver, or police, or photographers, and one of the Princes of Mardivino being discovered with an air-hostess bent busily over his lap.

Lucy flushed and moved away, suddenly feeling cheap as she imagined how it would look to an outsider. *Woman gets off plane and lets man ravish her in car.* A man, moreover, who had never made any promises of commitment to her and never would. Was she valuing herself too low—and, if so, for just how long was she going to let it continue?

'*Cara?*'

His voice was soft, and in anyone else you might almost be fooled into thinking that it was tender—but tenderness was an alien concept to Guido.

He saw the way that her eyes clouded and some stubborn inner resistance suddenly melted away. He leaned forward so that their foreheads were touching and began to stroke her hair.

'Forgive me, Lucy,' he said softly.

Lucy closed her eyes. For what? For taking her to heaven in an indecently short space of time? Or for drumming home the fact that where sex was concerned he was very definitely the master and she the puppet?

She opened her eyes again. 'You make me feel helpless,' she admitted.

He shrugged. 'Sometimes a woman should be helpless.'

'But not a man?' she questioned provocatively.

'Of course not.' His eyes sparked back in answering challenge. 'It is why we were born the stronger sex—did you not know that? We're conditioned to fight wars and to hunt—not to roll over on our backs like tame little pussycats.'

'Like I've just done, you mean?'

He brushed his lips against hers. 'Mmm. You were quite perfect. I like to see you like that.'

'Oh, you're just a power-freak,' she said, half crossly.

A smile curved his mouth. 'But you like that, too.'

'Sometimes.' Not always. Sometimes she would give a hundred erotic highs just to see him show even the briefest flicker of vulnerability—but that would be like wishing for the sky to suddenly start raining diamonds instead of hailstones. 'Sometimes I wish you'd just relax a bit more.'

'I'll relax later,' he promised silkily, and pulled her into the cradle of his arms. 'I promise you.'

'I don't just mean in bed,' said Lucy primly. 'It may be an alien concept to you, Guido, but you are allowed to let your hair down at other times.'

'Shh. Enough. That is enough, *cara*.'

Lucy rested her head against his shoulder and lapsed into a silence that was just the wrong side of contentment as she registered his unspoken reprimand. Was she nagging him? She stared out of the window just as the expensive car purred its way up Park Avenue and came to a halt in front of a rather beautiful old building.

She turned back to find his eyes watching her intently. 'Why are we stopping here?'

'Because we've arrived.'

Behind the Titian swing of her fringe, Lucy knitted her eyebrows together. 'This doesn't look like a hotel!'

'That's because it isn't.' He smiled, as if nothing was at stake. But something was, and they both knew it. 'I thought you might like to see my apartment.'

CHAPTER TWO

LUCY could read nothing in the ebony glitter of Guido's eyes, and somehow she kept her own expression casual—even though, deep down, she felt slightly shell-shocked. Guido wanted to take her home! Well, to *one* of his homes, that would be more accurate. At last. Now, why would that be?

'Your apartment?' she questioned slowly.

Not the kind of rapturous excitement he might have expected—which just went to show that in life you should expect nothing. 'Wouldn't you like to see it?'

She smiled at him. 'Of course I would.'

Up until now they'd always stayed in hotels—a city-central room was one of the perks of her flying job and, as a fabulously successful property developer, Guido rented luxury suites all over the world. In New York and in Paris he did actually own an apartment, but Lucy had seen neither.

To be allowed to set foot inside her boyfriend's home shouldn't have felt like a major achievement, but somehow it did. Was that what happened when you went out with a man like Guido? she wondered. You began to normalise abnormal behaviour?

He bent to retrieve her hat from the floor of the limousine. 'Want me to put it on for you?'

She felt her cheeks growing pink as she shook her

18

head. 'I hate that hat,' she said, more fervently than her opinion on a hat really warranted, but she could read the expression in his eyes perfectly well. He was remembering how she had come to lose the hat, and what had happened subsequently, and despite her reservations already she could feel the renewed rush of desire.

'It looks *très chic* on you,' he whispered. And then, because he wanted her very badly, he took her hand and kissed it. 'Come. Let us go inside. The driver will bring your bags.'

'Are you quite sure about this?' she murmured, as they rode up in the elevator towards the penthouse.

Actually, Guido had suffered a couple of reservations—until he'd told himself that he was in danger of becoming some fabled recluse. And he knew instinctively that he could trust Lucy not to gossip about his home.

Idly, he stroked his finger along the indentation of her waist. 'I want someone to sample my cooking.'

This time Lucy couldn't hide her surprise as she tried and failed spectacularly to imagine him in the kitchen. 'You mean you *cook*?'

'Actually, no, I don't.' His black eyes gleamed. 'Do you?'

Lucy nodded solemnly. 'Oh, yes. I adore cooking. In fact, I adore waiting on men in general. So I do hope you'll let me run round after you just as soon as we get there. You will, won't you, Guido?'

It took about three seconds for him to register the sarcastic note in her voice, and he pulled her into his arms. 'You are a wicked witch of a woman, Lucy Maguire,' he growled, and began to trail his lips over her cheek.

She closed her eyes, the raw and lemony feral scent of him invading her senses like a potent drug. The teasing comment pleased her, for in his voice she had heard the faintest note of puzzlement.

He couldn't work her out; she knew that—and she had actively encouraged it—but it was much more than a game to her. He closed himself off from her, so why should it fall on her shoulders to provide a one-way emotional show?

At the moment she had an air of mystery which he found alluring. If she allowed him to twitch that curtain of mystery aside, to let daylight come flooding in, then who knew what would happen?

She turned her head so that her lips brushed warm and soft and provocatively against his, and his eyes widened, surprising her with their hectic glitter.

'I want you,' he ground out.

'I should hope so, too,' she answered demurely.

'I want you so badly I could do it—'

'Here?' she pre-empted, brazenly cupping him once more. Only this time he didn't push her away. This time he groaned. She continued to trickle her fingers against his rock-hard shaft, pressing her lips close to his ear, as he had done to her at the airport. 'Do you want me to unzip you, Guido?' she questioned softly. 'To free you and then to slowly take you into my mouth? To lick my tongue up and down until you can hold back no longer and—'

He gave a roar like an angry lion as the lift pinged to a halt, buckling back the doors as if they were the enemy and unlocking his apartment, thanking God that he had had the foresight to dismiss all his staff for the rest of the day.

He slammed the door shut behind them, and Lucy—for all her carefully suppressed curiosity—didn't get a chance to notice any princely artefacts, for Guido was taking her by the hand in a way which broached no argument. But there again, who wanted to argue? Certainly not her.

He stopped short of actually kicking the bedroom door open, but his punch to it was so forceful that he might as well have done. Only when it was shut behind them did they stand facing one another, like two protagonists squaring up for a fight.

His breathing was laboured, and Lucy's heart was beating so rapidly that she felt faint. She was blind to the beauty of the New York skyline captured outside the enormous window—blind to anything other than the beauty of his face. She drank in the stark hunger which momentarily made his features look almost cruel, and the knowledge that she had him on a knife-edge of desire filled her with a sense of daring.

He had awoken in her a sense of passion and experimentation which not one of her other—laughably few—lovers had come even close to.

Or was it, mocked a small voice in her head, simply because he was such an accomplished and experienced lover that she felt she had to keep pushing back the boundaries in order to match him?

She put her hands on her hips and surveyed him from between slitted eyelids, her provocative pose at odds with the starchy, almost prim appearance of her navy blue uniform.

'Would you like me to strip for you...sir?' she questioned, in a tone of husky subservience.

Guido groaned. Could he bear to wait? And yet could he bear not to? For a man whose hunger had become jaded over years of having exactly what he wanted, this new and acutely keen appetite was something he wanted to savour.

For did not the sensation of hunger make you feel more alive than when you satisfied it? Had the blood ever sung in his veins quite as much as it was doing at the moment? Or the hard ache in his groin threatened to make him fall to the ground in front of her in complete surrender?

He nodded, not trusting himself to speak for a moment as he walked towards the giant bed and lay back against the pillows.

'Yes, strip,' he ordered curtly. 'Strip for me now.'

Lucy let out a sigh as her thumb and finger rubbed at the lapel of her jacket, caressing the material as sensuously as if it was skin. In a way, it was almost a relief to be able to play this game—for the game detracted from reality, and the reality was that Lucy suspected she was falling in love. Dangerous. Oh, so dangerous.

At least while she was acting the sultry siren she was able to stop herself from running over to him and cupping his hard, handsome face between her hands with a sense of wonder, then smothering it with tiny heartfelt kisses, telling him over and over that he made her heart sing and her senses come to vibrant and stinging life.

But that was not what he wanted from her. A man didn't have to spell it out for you that he was happy with just a casual affair, and Lucy was perceptive enough to have worked it out for herself in any case. And because she wanted to stay in the game she followed the rules that he had set. Did that make her weak? Or simply responsive?

Guido saw her hesitation and groaned, fighting back the urge to have her join him on the bed.

'Strip.' His voice rang out, the word a single, clipped command.

His voice was hard, she thought, but his eyes were as she had never seen them before—on fire with need and desire, and she had to steel herself against that look, to stop herself from melting. She slipped the jacket from her shoulders and hung it neatly over the back of a chair.

'Oh, Lucy,' he murmured.

She surveyed him steadily. 'Am I going too slowly for you, Guido?'

He heard the challenge in her voice. Say yes and she would take even longer! He shook his head, not daring—not able—to speak.

She began to undo the buttons of her crisp white shirt and saw him run his tongue over his lips as the garment joined her jacket. Slowly she unzipped the slim navy skirt and let it fall to the ground, so that it pooled by her feet. She stepped out of it. She heard his sharp inrush of breath as she stood before him, wearing just her bra and panties, stockings, suspender-belt and high navy shoes.

She undid the lace brassière and as it fell to the floor she began to touch her breasts, capturing his eyes with hers.

'Come here,' he whispered.

She shook her head. 'Not yet. Take your shirt off.'

His throat was dry as he peeled off the layer of ice-blue silk and threw it at her feet.

'Now your trousers,' she instructed softly. 'Take them off.'

His heart was crashing against his ribcage. 'Why don't *you* do it?' he murmured.

'Because I want you to.'

'Oh, do you?' he drawled.

He was aware that she was treating him as no woman had ever treated him before—and, rather more disturbingly, that he was *allowing her to*. But the sexual tension which was escalating second by frantic second was just too good and too powerful to resist.

In his highly aroused state he carefully slid off his trousers and briefs, watching with a certain mocking triumph as her eyes widened, her lips forming a pouting and moist little circle when she saw just how turned on he was.

'Oh, Guido,' she whispered, on a thready note of wonder.

Her fingertips moved from where they had been circling over her nipple to press between the juncture of her legs and her head fell back. She closed her eyes, and for a moment Guido wondered if she was just going to pleasure herself in front of him. And—in spite of his aching desire for her—wouldn't that be unbearably erotic to watch?

Driven on by an overwhelming need, he stroked his hand over himself as greedily as a schoolboy, and looked up to find her staring at him. Their eyes met in a moment of complete and silent understanding.

'Okay, Lucy,' he said unsteadily. 'You've played your little stripper game. That's enough. I want you here. Right now.'

His command was raw enough to make her forget the harsh note in his voice as he had said *stripper*. Her hands were trembling as she pulled her panties down and tossed them aside, and half-ran across the room towards him. And then she straddled him, easing herself down onto his hardness, squealing with delight as he filled her.

She thrust forward with her hips, as if she was riding bareback. But he rolled her straight over onto her back, assuming the position of mastery.

'Now,' he groaned, as he drove into her, over and over, each sweet, savage thrust sending her careering close to the edge. *'Now!'*

He bent his head to kiss her. The touch of his lips seemed to set fire to the touch-paper embedded deep in her heart and unstoppable flames began to flicker through her veins. She gave a broken little cry, but she bit down on it. She wanted to tell him that only he could make her feel this way. But for Guido this was simply good sex, and everyone knew that men could get good sex from any number of women.

And then the release washed over her—great powerful waves of it which rocked her to the very core, obliterating everything except the sheer wonder of the moment. Lucy clung to him, burying her face in his shoulder as he began to tense inside her, and to feel him beginning to orgasm only magnified her own pleasure.

For Guido it went on and on, and even when it was over he lay back, gazing dazedly at the ceiling. He couldn't remember sex as good as that. Never. He yawned, aware that his defences were down, irrevocably slipping into the dark, cushioned tunnel of sleep.

Lucy lay quite still until she heard Guido's breathing steady, then slow and deepen, and only when she was certain that he was asleep did she risk turning onto her side to look at him.

In sleep he was beautiful and curiously accessible in a way he never was while awake—making it impossible not to weave hopeless fantasies about him. Only in sleep did his hard and handsome face relax. The cruel, sensual mouth softened and the piercing brilliance of the ebony eyes was shielded by the feathery arcs of his lashes, which curved with such childlike innocence against his cheek.

His dark head was pillowed against a recumbent hand, and the long, lean limbs were sprawled over the giant-sized bed.

Lucy wriggled up the bed a bit, resting against a

bank of drift-soft pillows, and looked properly around the room for the first time.

So this was the Prince's bedroom!

There was little to mark it out as a Royal residence—it just looked like home to a very wealthy man. The bed was bigger than any she had ever seen, and the view from the window was utterly spectacular. No cost had been spared in the restrained but elegant furnishings. It was minimalist and unashamedly masculine, without in any way being hard or cold.

Only a silver-framed photo beside the bed gave any indication of his identity, and unless you knew it could have been any snapshot of any rich and privileged family.

But it was not.

It was a picture of Guido, taken with his mother, his elder brother Gianferro, and their father the King. Guido, with his black hair and black eyes, looked to be about four or five. Lucy bit her lip, moving her eyes over the figure of the beautiful young Queen. There was no outward sign of her pregnancy with Nicolo—the youngest—and certainly no sign that within a year of that photo being taken she would be dead. Thank God humans could not see into the future, she thought, with a sudden stab of pain.

She stared at the young Guido. In the face of the child it was possible to see the man. His face was sweetly handsome, his expression almost grave, as if he was determined to be a grown-up boy for the mother whose hand he gripped so tightly.

But Lucy had only learnt all this subsequently. It was easy to find out things about someone when you were interested—and when they were in the public eye. Not that she had known that he was a prince when she'd met him. At least, not at first.

To Lucy, he had been just a heart-stoppingly gorgeous man who had struck up a conversation with her at a party.

CHAPTER THREE

IT HAD been one of those parties that Lucy hadn't particularly wanted to go to—she had been on a stopover on her way back to London and desperate for some sleep—but the flight crew had overridden her objections. Apparently, parties didn't get much better or more highly connected than this one. One of the other stewardesses had said that a prince was going to be there, but quite honestly Lucy hadn't believed them.

Well, who would have?

When they had walked into the expensive Bohemian TriBeCa townhouse, Lucy had looked around her with interest. It had been like stepping into some lavishly appointed Bedouin tent—with embroidered cushions and rich brocade wall-hangings, and the heady scent of incense. The hypnotic drift of what had sounded like snake-charmer's music had only added to the illusion of being on a film set.

'When do the belly-dancers arrive?' she asked drily.

'Shh!' someone hissed. 'You know people tend to misunderstand your sense of humour!'

So Lucy decided to observe, rather than to participate, and went to stand in a darkened corner which nonetheless gave her a great view. She took a glass of punch with her and sipped it, then shuddered, hastily putting the glass down on a small inlaid table.

'Disgusting, isn't it?' came a rich, accented voice from a few feet away.

Lucy was just about to protest that he had startled her when her words somehow died on her lips. 'It's...a little heavy on the spices,' she agreed, blinking slightly, as if she couldn't quite believe what she was seeing.

'And the alcohol, of course.'

'Well, there is that, of course,' she echoed, and he smiled.

They stood looking at one another in the way that two people did at parties when there was a strong sexual chemistry between them.

Lucy was wearing a simple green velvet tunic dress—quite short, so that it came to mid-thigh and made her legs look endlessly long. But her baggy suede boots gave the outfit a quirky appearance. Her hair was loose, flooding down over her shoulders in a heavy Titian fall.

Guido thought that she looked like a very sexy bandit. Her face was pale and freckled—he liked the freckles—and her wide honey-coloured eyes were slightly wary—he liked that, too.

Lucy thought, quite honestly, that he was the most gorgeous man she had ever laid eyes on. But then, she had never seen a man who looked quite like this.

He was tall, and his body was both lean and powerful. His hair was as black as the night, and his eyes only a shade lighter, and he had an almost aristocratic bearing. She wondered if he was Italian, or maybe Spanish. He was certainly European.

And he almost certainly has a girlfriend, she told herself. If not one, then a legion of them.

Guido waited, but she said nothing, and he liked that even more. So, did she know? he wondered. And was she pretending not to? 'You're not from round here?' he questioned slowly.

'No.'

'You're on holiday?' he persisted.

'Not really. I work for Pervolo Airlines.'

'As a pilot?'

'You ask a lot of questions.'

His eyes glittered. 'One of us has to.'

Hers glittered back. 'I'm a flight attendant, actually—but thank you for not making the assumption.'

'Assumptions are such a bore, don't you think?' he questioned carelessly.

It was something about the way he spoke—some unknown quality underlying the velvet accent of his voice—which Lucy had difficulty recognising at first, because she had never heard it before. And then he gave her a silent clue in the proud way he was holding his head—in the dismissive little curve of his sensual mouth as a woman wearing so little that she might have been one of those belly-dancers started ogling him from the other side of the room.

It was privilege, Lucy realised. A sense of self-worth bordering on arrogance which radiated from him in a way which was almost tangible. Haughty, but with a devilish glitter to his eyes, he managed to

be both gloriously touchable and yet impossibly remote at the same time.

'You're the Prince,' said Lucy slowly, and she felt
the slightest pang of disappointment. Just her luck to
find someone who could have whisked her off her feet
and then discover he was out of bounds! 'Aren't
you?'

His eyes narrowed. 'You knew?'

Lucy shook her head. 'No. I've just guessed.
Someone said there was going to be a prince here,
but I didn't believe them.' Her eyes were candid.
'What a bore for you—that everyone knows about
you in advance.'

'The perfect catch for the ambitious society host-
ess,' he observed drily.

'Yes, quite.' So, was that arrogant? Or merely honest? Lucy expelled a sigh and gave him a small, regretful smile. She certainly wasn't going to fill the
stereotypical role of hanging around and being star-
struck. 'Well, it was nice meeting you—'

'But we haven't, have we?' he said suddenly. 'Met,
that is. Perhaps we should remedy that?' His smile
was irresistible, and so was his voice, and he took her
hand in his without warning. 'I'm Guido.'

'Lucy,' she said breathlessly. His touch was sending her senses haywire. 'Lucy Maguire—but you'd
better let me go—I don't want to monopolise you.'

'Liar,' he taunted softly, his fingers continuing to
curl possessively around her narrow wrist. 'You know
we both want to monopolise each other.'

'How outrageous!' she murmured, but she didn't move from the spot.

They talked all night. She was simultaneously lulled and stimulated by his quicksilver mind and sexy accent. He came from the Principality of Mardivino, but he had long ago rejected princely privilege. 'Perhaps you find that disappointing?' he mocked.

'I thought you weren't into making assumptions,' she returned crisply. 'Because that was an extremely arrogant one.'

'You sound like a prim schoolteacher,' he observed sultrily. 'Even if you do not look like one.'

Lucy raised her eyebrows but said nothing—certainly not anything that was going to lead into the tantalising land of sexual fantasy.

'So, what do princes do?' she questioned. 'When they're not being princes?'

'Oh, they wheel and deal,' he murmured, drifting his gaze over her freckle-spattered face. 'Just like other mortals.'

She didn't think so. Other mortals did not have the faces of dark fallen angels. 'A-anything in particular?' she stammered—because when he was looking at her like that it was difficult to breathe, let alone to speak.

'Property,' he said succinctly.

He offered to give her a lift back to her hotel, but Lucy refused—though she let him flag her down a cab. She wasn't sure she trusted his unique brand of sexy charisma enough to be alone in a car with him—

or maybe it was that she didn't trust herself not to respond to it.

He leaned into the cab and handed her his card.

'Why don't you ring me when you're next in town?' he suggested softly.

Lucy smiled politely and took the card, but the smile was edged in a frost he appeared not to notice. She got the distinct impression that he felt he was bestowing an enormous favour on her by giving her a contact number. Bloody cheek!

She didn't bother ringing. His arrogance had disappointed her, yes—but it was more than that. He was a prince, for heaven's sake—and thus completely out of her reach. Only someone with a streak of masochism would willingly subject themselves to such inevitable rejection.

But Guido, of course, had never before been ignored by a woman.

At first he simply couldn't believe that she wasn't going to bother to ring. But after several weeks he had no choice but to do so.

Why, he couldn't even remember her surname!

But that, of course, did not pose any real problem. Guido had left his life as a working prince behind a long time ago, but very occasionally he used his title. He still had to exist with all the drawbacks of having it, he reasoned—so why not enjoy some of the benefits?

And Pervolo Airlines seemed only too happy to release a few facts about one of their stewardesses to a prince!

He found out when she was next flying and settled back in his seat in First Class, anticipating her reaction with a certain degree of relish, feeling himself grow deliciously hard as he saw a pair of long, long legs slinking down the cabin towards him.

Lucy had noticed him, of course—it would have been difficult not to, even if they hadn't already been briefed by the Purser that there was a Royal prince on board.

But she had no intention of reacting to the look of appreciation which had softened the ebony eyes. She had no desire to be just another notch on a handsome, privileged man's bedpost, and she was perceptive enough to know that this man could be a real heart-breaker.

She reached him, her face set in an unflappable, official smile. 'Good afternoon, sir,' she said pleasantly. 'Can I get you a drink before take-off?'

He had been expecting…what? That she would blush and stumble over her words? Look regretful or uncomfortable? Suddenly he laughed, and his pulse began to race.

'No, you can have dinner with me tonight instead,' he murmured, and some of his arrogance dissolved as he stared up at her. 'Please.'

Lucy would have defied anyone to resist that look, or the one-word plea she guessed he hadn't had to make very often in his life. So she went for dinner with him, and then—after not much of a fight—to bed. She wanted him more than she had ever wanted anything in her life, and to hold him off any longer would have been hypocritical and self-defeating.

But, despite the passion of the night which followed, an instinctive feeling of self-protection made her noncommittal towards him the next morning. She was determined not to seem pushy, or to act as if it would be the end of the world if he didn't ask to see her again, and her very coolness seemed to fascinate him.

She guessed he'd never encountered it before, and to a man with an appetite jaded by exposure it was fresh and exciting fare. Soon it would no longer be fresh, nor exciting, and it would pale, but she was prepared for that—or at least that was what she told herself over and over again.

Apart from a minor blip at the very beginning, they now met up once every couple of months and it was perfect—for what it was. They had dinner, sometimes saw a film, and once or twice he had taken her to the theatre. But she had never met any of his friends, nor he hers. It was a complex game they played, with its own set of unspoken rules. As if she had been given her own separate compartment in his life—the one marked 'mistress'—and as long as she accepted that, then she was okay. The moment she started wanting more, then it would be over.

So why had he brought her to his apartment today? Why not the usual anonymity of a hotel?

She stared down at his sleeping face just as the dark lashes fluttered open and ebony eyes blazed sleepily up at her.

'*Ciao,*' he murmured, and reached for her breast. 'Come back here.'

'In a minute.' She let him stroke idly at her breast as warmth began to flood over her. If he had broken a rule of a lifetime, then why shouldn't she? Lucy trickled her fingertip down through the thick whorls of hair at his chest to dip it into his belly, and he groaned with pleasure. 'How flattering that you have allowed me onto your territory, Guido,' she commented softly.

'Why not?' His eyes were watchful black shards. 'Though you've never shown any particular desire to see where I live.'

'Ah.' She raised her eyebrows. And presumably if she had then his apartment would have been off-limits! 'Interesting.'

How her self-containment enthralled and exasperated him! Why, any other woman would have used his post-coital sleep as an opportunity to poke around the apartment! Yet here she was, naked and beautiful beside him, as though she visited his home every day of the week!

He narrowed his eyes as he felt the heavy throb of desire beating its way through his veins. As a lover, he could not have asked for better. She was responsive and beautiful and she made no demands on him. How unlike most women!

His mouth hardened as he thought about commitment and expectation. And, in particular, about the lavish christening of his nephew, soon to take place on Mardivino, and all that it would entail. He stared at the naked woman beside him and an idea began to form in his mind. Maybe her cool indifference could work to his advantage...

'Would you like to go away with me for the week-end, *cara mia*?' he suggested casually.

Lucy didn't answer immediately—it was never a good idea to appear *too* eager; every woman knew *that*! 'Did you have anywhere particular in mind?'

'But of course.' His eyes glittered as he wondered what her reaction would be. For if she read too much into it then it simply would not work. 'I thought that perhaps you might care to accompany me to Mardivino.'

There was silence as, for a minute, Lucy thought she was hearing things. 'To Mardivino?' she repeated blankly.

'Do try to contain your excitement,' he commented drily.

Oh, if only he knew! Lucy's heart was banging against her ribcage and she felt quite faint. He was taking her home—to meet his family!

A slow smile curved her lips. 'And to what do I owe this honour?'

Guido concentrated on whispering his fingertips over her tightening nipple. 'Maybe I'd like to show you the land of my birth,' he murmured.

Lucy closed her eyes, partly because the way he was touching her meant that she could barely think straight, but partly to hide her eyes. To conceal from him the breathless excitement she was feeling.

Don't frighten him away with emotion, she told

herself, sinking into his arms. Let's just take it one step at a time.

'Okay,' she said lightly, as if it didn't matter. *As if it didn't matter!* 'Why not?'

He smiled with satisfaction at her response. It was better than he could have anticipated! 'And maybe I would like a beautiful woman to accompany me to the christening of my nephew.'

There was a long pause as Lucy stared up at him. 'Say that again.'

'My brother's child is being baptised. Would you like to come?'

She blinked her eyes very quickly. A baptism was a private and very sacred thing, and he was asking her...*her*... 'Are you...are you sure?'

'I wouldn't ask you unless I was.' He ran a fingertip reflectively down over the bare silk of her shoulder. 'You will need something to wear, of course. We shall go shopping later, yes?'

It was as if someone had given her a gorgeous present and then snatched it away again, and Lucy froze. 'You're saying that you don't think I have anything suitable?'

There was not a flicker of reaction on his face. '*Cara*, you always look *meravigliosa*.'

'So what's the problem?'

'There is no problem.' He chose his words carefully. 'But it will be—of necessity—a very lavish affair,' he said slowly. 'And I would like to buy you an outfit.'

'You think I'm going to turn up in jeans and a sweatshirt?' she demanded.

'Of course I don't!'

'Well, then—I can buy my own outfits,' she said stubbornly.

'Yes, I know you can.' He moved his head away to look down at her, his black eyes like jet as he chose his words in a way calculated not to offend her sweet but misplaced pride. 'Let me put it another way,' he said softly. 'You are my lover, Lucy, and tradition dictates that as my lover I am allowed to spoil you. I *want* to spoil you,' he added huskily.

And this, too, was all part of the game, she realised. If she accompanied him then it was imperative that she look the part. It didn't matter if she dressed with style and panache—her budget was far too limited to allow her to be able to compete with other women at a Royal gathering.

And she wanted to go. Badly. If she allowed stubborn pride to rear its head then he might refuse to take her. And if she held out to wear one of her own outfits—then wasn't there a chance she might let him down?

Besides—if she was being one hundred per cent honest—then wasn't there a wistful Cinderella side to *every* woman—that wanted someone to wave a magic wand and transform them from an ordinary woman into a princess? Well, that was just what Guido was offering to do, and as long as she didn't expect the Cinderella ending then why not just go with the flow and enjoy it? What else was she going to do? Tell him no and have the relationship peter out?

The thought of that hurt far more than she wanted or had expected, and she shrugged her shoulders, as if the unwelcome stab of reality wasn't poking brittle fingers at her heart. 'Very well, Guido,' she said slowly. 'I accept.'

'You test me, I think, *cara*,' he observed evenly.

'Oh?'

'A man does not offer a gift to have it treated as though it is some kind of punishment to be endured.'

'A gift should be offered without ties or expectations,' she returned sweetly. 'Didn't you know that?'

'Do you always have a smart answer for everything, Lucy?'

'I certainly hope so.' She narrowed her eyes. 'If it is submissive gratitude you desire, Guido, then there must be any number of women who would be only too glad to provide it.'

And she was right, *maledizione*! He enjoyed much more than just her lovemaking because she challenged and intrigued him—he could not now dispense with those qualities when it suited him.

He put his hand between her thighs and heard her gasp. 'I am going to make love to you again,' he said, on a note of husky intent. 'And then I am going to take you out and dress you from head to foot.'

Lucy let him whisk her around Manhattan, unable to shake the slightly surreal sensation of feeling as though she was appearing in a film as Guido took her from shop to exclusive shop. Stuff like this didn't happen in real life, she told herself dazedly.

But it seemed that it did.

First came the lingerie—stuff like she had never seen before: drifts and drifts of delicate silk, trimmed with lace so fine that it seemed to have been spun from gossamer. A brisk, efficient Frenchwoman measured her, and it transpired that Lucy had been buying the wrong bra size off the peg for years!

'We'll take them both,' drawled Guido carelessly as she vascillated between a matching set in electric blue trimmed with cerise satin and a more conventional pure white outfit—which was, she thought with a fleeting wistfulness, exactly the kind of thing a bride might covet for her trousseau. 'And the black.'

'Guido, no!' protested Lucy as the saleswoman tactfully withdrew from the room.

'Guido, yes,' he argued, with a smile of satisfaction.

'I won't be wearing more than two sets of underwear in a weekend!'

'But after the weekend you will, and I want to see you in it all. And out of it,' he said, his voice dipping into a note of erotic promise.

Of course she couldn't possibly argue after that—because his words implied that their affair was going to run and run when they got back from Mardivino.

She silenced the cruel little voice in her head which asked her just how long she was prepared to dedicate her life to a relationship which was doomed to go nowhere.

In a succession of luxurious shops he bought her an outfit for the christening, plus the most gorgeous hat she had ever seen, two evening gowns, daywear, negligees, and a cashmere wrap.

'Sometimes the evening breeze which comes down from the mountains can chill the skin,' he murmured. 'Especially skin as fine and as fair as yours, Lucy.'

He ran his fingers lightly over her bare arm and Lucy began to tremble. Tersely he asked for the garments to be wrapped and delivered and then took her back to his apartment and made love to her all over again. He was wild for it, and so was she, and the sound of her ecstatic cries rang round his vast bedroom as she lay shuddering in his arms afterwards.

But once the storms of passion had abated Lucy felt different. Something had changed, or at least in her imagination it had, and she wondered if she had given away something of herself in her shamefully easy acceptance of his gifts. Her independence, maybe?

She snuggled into the crook of his arm, for he was sleeping, and her own eyelids began to drift down.

I will only wear the clothes on Mardivino, she vowed.

And after that I'll go back to being me.

CHAPTER FOUR

'LOOK down now,' said Guido, above the sound of the engines. 'And you will see the mountains of Mardivino.'

Lucy did as he said, though she was so distracted by his proximity that she might as well have been looking at the skyscrapers of a city for all the impact the breathtaking scenery made on her.

Was it the fact they were now most definitely moving into *his* exclusive territory that was making her feel very slightly disorientated—or just the rather daunting prospect of what might lie ahead? With an effort she forced herself not to think about the sexy and sophisticated Prince who sat beside her on the luxury jet, and to drink in the beauty of his homeland instead.

Beneath her lay a bewitching-looking island which sparkled like a jewel set in a blindingly blue sea. In the distance she could see the mighty peaks of the mountains he had mentioned, and as the plane circled she could see beaches and brilliant white buildings clustered together, like a handful of pearls.

'Wow!' she breathed. 'Is that a city there?'

He smiled. 'It's Solajoya—our capital. I don't know if it qualifies as a city, as it's pretty small— though it *does* have a cathedral.'

'Then it's a city,' said Lucy firmly.

Guido leaned over her to stare down. How long since he had been back? He had paid fleeting visits to see his father, of course, but he had not been back since his younger brother Nico had surprised them all and married the English girl.

At first it had been considered the most unsuitable of liaisons, and Guido had been expecting an explosive firework response from his elder brother Gianferro. But Ella seemed to have won him round, and Gianferro—against all the odds—had accepted her into the bosom of the family. And now she had secured her place there permanently, by giving Nico a son and heir.

His mouth hardened. Even Nico—the wild and devil-may-care Nico—had succumbed to the expectations which were his birthright!

He stared at Lucy's smooth cheek and the sweep of glossy Titian hair which contrasted so beautifully against it. Yes. She would make a very enjoyable deterrent against the subtle pressure of the Palace to settle down at last, with a suitable bride. Her presence at his side would shield him from the attentions of Mardivino's maritally ambitious women. His lips curved into a smile. And—best of all—he could relax and enjoy just about the best sex he'd ever had in his life.

'Excited?' he questioned softly.

Lucy nodded, because there seemed to be some kind of lump in her throat preventing normal speech. Excited? Well, yes—if excitement also incorporated sheer terror. She had always thought of herself as adaptable, and her job had taken her to all kinds of places to meet all kinds of people—but there was nothing in any rule book to tell her how to deal with a situation like this.

For a start, she didn't *feel* like herself—nor even look like herself, either. The pale linen trousers were cut low on the hip and were the most flattering pair of trousers she had ever worn. You got—as everyone always said—what you paid for, and Guido had paid a hell of a lot for these! They were teamed with a T-shirt which didn't really look like a T-shirt—its fit was so perfect that it seemed to take what should have been an everyday garment into a completely new dimension.

And beneath the expensive clothes were equally expensive undergarments—silk and satin which glided like honey over her curves and which managed to make her feel very sexy indeed.

Not that there was much point in feeling *that*, because Guido had been as untactile as it was possible to be ever since they had boarded the private jet.

She could understand it—but that didn't make it any easier. He was on show now—to the two pilots and the unbelievably beautiful stewardess, as well as to all the officials who had fussed them onto the plane. He might have rejected life as a prince, but that didn't mean he wouldn't conform to it when he needed to. That was simply good manners and aristocratic breeding.

Consequently, he hadn't touched her, nor kissed

her, nor even murmured provocatively in her ear, promising what he was going to do to her in bed later—not once, during the entire flight.

He had been cool almost to the point of being indifferent, and that had scared her—because it seemed to reinforce what she knew in her heart. He might like her enough to bring her here for the weekend, and he might like going to bed with her, but he certainly didn't love her—and therefore it was vital she didn't fall in any deeper than she already was.

So how did you stop yourself falling in love?

She looked out at the clouds which drifted like dry ice past the windows. What would she do if she knew that there was a bad case of flu going around? She would go out of her way to protect herself. She should do the same with her emotions. Enjoy the weekend for what it was.

The engine noise changed and the plane began to dip down towards the tiny airport. Lucy smoothed her hair back, hoping that the gesture didn't look nervous.

'Will anyone be there to meet us?' she questioned.

'Just a driver. I told my brother not to send a deputation.'

'Did he want to, then?'

Guido gave a hard smile. 'Gianferro likes pomp and ceremony—which is fortunate, since he's going to have a hell of a lot of it one of these days.'

Lucy hesitated. 'How is…your father?'

'He is slowly dying,' said Guido matter-of-factly, and he saw her flinch. But how could he explain that being pragmatic was his way of dealing with it? He had learnt early on about the finality and pain of death when his mother had been torn away from her family. Nico had been just a baby and Gianferro—as the oldest and the heir—had always been surrounded and protected by an extra layer of courtiers.

But Guido had been at the worst possible age for maternal deprivation, which was probably why they had flown him to stay with his mother's sister in America. He had loved his aunt very much, but she had not been his mother, and away from his brothers and Mardivino his sense of lonelieness and isolation had increased.

And when he had returned it had not felt like home any more.

No place had ever since.

A low black limousine was waiting on the runway, and it whisked them off to a palace which Lucy hadn't imagined could exist outside the pages of a fairy story.

'The Rainbow Palace,' said Guido, as the mosaic building glittered in the distance in a multicoloured dazzle.

'It's so beautiful,' breathed Lucy. 'Is this where you were born?'

'It is,' he said curtly.

'And where did you go to school?'

'I didn't. We had tutors at the Palace.'

So he would have been cut off from the outside world—in the same way that he now seemed to have cut himself off from the island itself.

Lucy sneaked a glance at him. His dark profile was

hard and noncommittal as the gates opened and the car swept through onto a vast forecourt which was studded with beautiful statues and bright with tropical flowers.

'Do your brothers mind me coming?' she asked him hesitantly.

There wasn't a flicker of reaction on his face. Nico had been interested—rather *too* interested, in Guido's opinion—and had quizzed him about actually bringing a woman with him to Mardivino until Guido had set him straight. He had told his younger brother that Lucy was his lover—nothing more and nothing less. 'Don't start writing hearts and flowers,' he had said wryly. 'Just because you've fallen in love yourself.'

Gianferro had been a different matter altogether— stating flatly that it was unthinkable for Guido to bring a woman to the Palace if she was merely a casual consort.

There had been a hot-headed exchange about this use of terminology, with Guido telling Gianferro that he was a modern, urban man who didn't go along with such a derogatory description of a woman.

Gianferro had gone to great pains to try to explain himself. 'I am not trying to insult this…Lucy,' he had said exasperatedly. 'But while you may consider yourself a "modern, urban man" you are still a prince. I am afraid that I cannot countenance the idea of you cohabiting with her on Mardivino.'

Knowing that he held all the cards, Guido had responded coolly. 'Then I shall not come.'

'That is unthinkable!'

'Precisely.'

It didn't matter how much Gianferro raged, on this Guido had been adamant—not only would he be bringing Lucy, but he wanted them to share a suite of rooms at the Palace.

'I am not going to behave like a seventeen-year-old schoolboy!' he had stormed. 'Sneaking into her room late at night.'

'Think of your birthright!' his brother had retorted.

'I do—constantly! I have chosen to live my life by my own rules, and I am asking you to respect that.'

He looked now into Lucy's honey-coloured eyes and gave a thin smile. 'No,' he said lightly. 'My brothers do not mind you coming.'

He supposed that some people might have called this a distortion of the truth, but in his world he would prefer to define it as diplomacy. Sometimes it was better all round if you told people what they wanted to hear.

The luxury car purred to a halt and various servants appeared from within the ornate doors of the Palace. As Lucy stepped out of the car, to feel the sun beating down on her bare head, the feeling of being in a dream was stronger than ever.

Guido was speaking to one of the servants in low and rapid French, while others were removing their baggage and taking it inside. He turned to her and his black eyes glittered.

'Shall we go to our rooms?' he suggested casually. 'You might wish to change.' His eyes glittered. 'And my brother Gianferro would like to meet you before we go down to dinner.'

It was not a question, Lucy realised, it was an order—subtly and charmingly couched, but an order nonetheless. As much as Guido might declare that he had left his Royal life behind, it was ingrained in his psyche, running as deep as an underground river. You couldn't escape your upbringing—leave it behind and forget it—simply because you wanted to.

On Mardivino he would inevitably be the Prince, and as his lover Lucy had her own part to play. So play the part, she told herself, but don't let the barriers slip—not by a fraction.

She remembered what Gary, her house-mate, had told her before she left: 'Everyone will love you! Just be yourself, darling!'. But what did that actually mean? That she should let rip with her feelings? Not in this case, no. She suspected that it was more a case of being natural and easy-going—in other words being the perfect guest. She would go along with everything and drink in the experience of a lifetime.

'Sounds wonderful,' she agreed equably.

Guido took her to their suite via a maze of wide marble corridors, hung with spectacular oil paintings, and then through an inner courtyard which was cool and scented, with a fountain sprinkling water which sounded like music.

He stood watching her for a moment as she sucked in a deep breath of wonder, for it was impossible not to be awed by such beauty.

'You like it,' he observed.

Lucy turned to face him, seeing the shuttered look in his black eyes. 'Don't you?'

He shrugged. 'I grew up here. You always look at things differently from the inside. And memories change how you view something.'

She heard the rawness in his voice. Had his bereaved and fractured childhood caused scars which could never be healed? But to ask him would be intrusive, even if he were the kind of man who invited such questions. And Lucy did not want to pry, or to add to his pain. There were other ways of telling someone that you understood.

'I know what you mean,' she said thoughtfully. 'It's like if you live by the sea—you get so used to seeing it that you take it for granted.' Her mouth twitched. 'And I guess that nothing can prepare you for growing up in the kind of place that most mortals pay ticket money to see!'

There was a pause, and then, unexpectedly, he began to laugh. His social status was so lofty that rarely did people tease him about it—though when he stopped to think about it rarely did he *let* anyone tease him.

His laughter broke some of the tension and replaced it with a new, much more acceptable kind. He stared at her. In the linen trousers and clinging T-shirt she looked like a sleeker and more expensive version of the usual Lucy. As if he had upgraded from a run-of-the-mill car to something top-of-the-range.

Had he tried to alter her? So that the woman he

admired and lusted after would now slip away, like sand between his fingers?

Suddenly he wanted to see her naked, stripped of all the finery that he had insisted on dressing her in.

'Let's go to our suite, *cara*,' he said unsteadily.

She knew exactly what he wanted to do from the look in his eyes, but she was hardly going to challenge him in the public arena of the Palace courtyard. Or rather she sensed that it was public—there was no one to be seen, but she could not shake off the idea that there were eyes watching them.

Maybe they have closed-circuit TV installed, she thought, with a slight touch of hysteria.

She barely had a chance to take in the sumptuous ice-blue and golden surroundings of their suite, for Guido pulled her into his arms, pressing his hard, lean body against hers. She felt the unmistakable evidence of his desire for her, and the melting response of her answering need.

'Guido,' she breathed against his ear as he began to tug at the waistband of her trousers and slide his hand inside them. 'We mustn't.'

'Mustn't what?' he questioned, his eyes gleaming like some dark, indefinable metal as he watched her pupils dilate, felt her syrupy moistness as he began to move his finger.

She closed her eyes, her knees growing weak. 'Your brother...' she gasped. 'He'll be waiting.'

The trousers pooled in a whisper by her ankles and he gave an unseen smile of triumph.

'And so, *cara*,' he said harshly, 'am I. And I can wait no longer!'

It all happened very quickly. He divested her of her costly garments, flinging them carelessly onto the floor as if they were of no consequence, and Lucy suddenly felt like a mannequin he could clothe and then unclothe whenever the fancy took him. As if she were his possession. And she was *not*!

Damn you, she thought. *Damn* you, Prince Guido Nero Maximus Cacciatore, with your cavalier attitude and your determination to get just what it is you want!

But didn't she want it, too? Oh, so badly…

She tugged viciously at his silk shirt, so that several buttons popped off, skittering and bouncing on the marble floor, and she heard him give a low laugh of delight as she scraped her fingernails against the dark hair which arrowed down over his torso.

'Lucy,' he moaned.

His sound of helpless pleasure fuelled her on, and somehow they made it to the bed, frantically pulling at their remaining clothes.

Lucy's breathing was frantic as she began to straddle him. 'Have you…have you locked the door?' she demanded, her voice shaking.

'*Si!*'

Sweet saints in heaven! His one word of assent was enough to have her lowering herself down on him, playing with him, easing the tip of him against her and then seeming to hesitate, as though she was about to change her mind.

'Lucy—' he begged, gasping with the exquisite

pleasure of it as she sank down onto him, taking in every bit of him, and he was so full, so tight, that he felt he might burst.

He buried his face in her breasts as she began to move, taunting and tormenting him as she changed the rhythm until he could bear it no longer. He caught her by the hips, increasing the speed, watching with pleasure as her eyes became slitted and her head fell back and she hissed out the word *yes* over and over and over again, until all his seed had pumped deep within her.

He shook his head slightly with disbelief and sank back against the rumpled pillows, pulling her sweat-sheened body against him. He wanted to sleep, but she was shaking him, her face all flushed and her silken hair falling about her pale freckled shoulders.

'Guido—wake up!'

He shook his head and wriggled his hips comfortably.

She touched the damp silken skin which covered the hard musculature of his shoulder. 'Didn't you say we had to see your brother?'

Reluctantly he opened his eyes, swearing quietly as he lifted his wrist to glance at his watch and then at her. With her tumble of tousled hair and the hectic glitter of her honey-coloured eyes she looked exactly what she was. A highly-sexed and wanton woman who had just been ravished. He felt himself harden, wishing himself far away from the constrictions of this old life again. What wouldn't he give to do it to her all over again?

'How soon can you be ready?' The question came out more tersely than he had intended, but he was trying desperately to detach himself—and for once it wasn't easy. Was that because she was the most equal lover he had ever had?

Lucy blushed, her already high colour deepening still further. 'I'll need to take a quick shower,' she said. 'And I'll have to get something from my suit-case. To wear,' she added.

'Some of your clothes will have already been hung up,' he said shortly. 'The rest are being pressed. Hurry up now, *cara mia*. The bathroom is through there.'

Still shaky, she moved away from the bed and stumbled towards the door he was indicating.

Lucy had been flying long enough to be able to get ready in fast time, but as she stood beneath the power jets of the shower it occurred to her that there had not really been time for what had just happened. He should have stopped. She had tried to stop him—not very hard, it was true—but she had done her level best.

Was it an act of defiance? Or some basic and ter-ritorial instinct that had made Guido want to make love to her so passionately and so immediately?

She was so busy selecting what on earth she should wear to go and meet the Crown Prince, and wonder-ing why he had requested to meet her before dinner, that a vital fact completely slipped her mind.

CHAPTER FIVE

'His Serene Highness the Crown Prince Gianferro Miguel Laurens Cacciatore.'

Lucy rose to her feet as Guido's imposing brother entered the room, aware that her pulse was racing and her mouth dry.

It was strange—though understandable, she supposed—that she had always been remarkly unfazed by Guido's title and position, yet she felt positively nervous about meeting the heir to the throne for the first time. Maybe it was because she had met Guido socially, at a party, when he could have been just anyone—whilst here, in the Palace, she felt rather as she imagined a small child might feel if they had been chosen out of all their classmates to present a bouquet to the Queen.

Even though Guido had told her not to, she found herself making some kind of bobbing curtsey, and he nodded in response, a rather reluctant smile curving his lips.

'Please,' he said, and indicated a chair close to the rather more ornate one he had perched on. 'Sit.' He glanced at his brother. 'Guido, you will leave us?'

Guido gave an equable nod which belied the cold gleam of anger in his eyes. 'I'll stay. Lucy likes to have me around—do you not, *cara*?'

Lucy had a brother of her own, and she recognised sibling rivalry and unsettled scores when she came across them. The two men were glaring at each other across the Throne Room and she felt like piggy-in-the-middle. This was hardly going to bode well for the baptism—unless she could manage to turn it around so that neither man lost face.

'Yes, Guido,' she said softly, 'I do. But I'm happy to speak with your brother alone if you think I can manage it?'

Guido's eyes narrowed as they engaged in a silent, clashing duel with hers. Now she was making it sound as though he was watching over her to ensure that she did not make some monumental error of manners, leaving him no choice but to withdraw. He scowled. Why did women always play such complicated games?

'I will go and say hello to my new nephew,' he said abruptly, and shot his brother a mocking glance. 'Perhaps you would care to direct Lucy to the nursery, Gianferro, once you've finished your little…chat?'

Gianferro nodded. '*Si.*' But when Guido had left the room he turned to Lucy, a curious expression in the black eyes which were even harder than Guido's. 'How strange it is,' he observed, in a softly accented voice which seemed underpinned with a note of censure, 'that my brothers seem attracted to women who are light-years away from them in upbringing and experience.'

She didn't think he had meant to insult her, but an insult it undoubtedly was—though one couched in silken terms. *You are not Guido's equal.* That was what he really meant, and Lucy stared at him. Did he think she didn't already know that? That she hadn't been aware of the great and glaring differences right from the word go? Yet pride made her want to hang on to her dignity, not to state the obvious and pick over her humble background.

Her training as a stewardess had given her an invaluable lesson in the making of small-talk, and she seized on it now. 'Perhaps they enjoy variety,' she said lightly.

His eyes narrowed, as if he suspected that she had deliberately misunderstood him. He paused for a moment, and when he spoke the silken veneer of his words had been replaced with the harder ring of truth. 'I understand that you have been seeing him for almost a year.'

'Did Guido tell you that?' she asked in surprise.

'Not exactly.'

And Lucy recognised then that whatever Guido did his movements would be monitored and fed back to the Crown Prince. No doubt Gianferro would have said that he had Guido's best interests at heart, but wasn't it really a not-so-subtle method of spying?

Suddenly she felt protective of her lover. And defensive, too. 'We meet only infrequently,' she said quickly. 'Because of the nature of my job.'

'And *his* nature.'

Their eyes met. Now he was telling her that Guido was not the settling-down type, and once again his words were redundant. For she knew that, too. 'Perhaps,' she said slowly.

'So it is a modern relationship?' he continued softly. 'You are simply lovers?'

She would certainly never have described them as 'simple', yet couldn't help the smile which broke out briefly, like the sun through watery clouds. 'Indeed we are.'

There was another brief silence, and then he said, so casually that it might have been a careless throwaway remark had it not been for the questioning glitter of his dark eyes, 'And you do not hold out some hope that one day you will become a Princess of Mardivino?'

Lucy was stung by the slur, which implied that she was socially ambitious, that she had no feelings for Guido himself—and, God knows, she did. Even though a deep, self-protective streak had made her do her best to quash them. Yet her own feelings paled into insignificance beside the realisation of just how stifling Royal life could be. No wonder Guido had rejected it!

Her words came blurting out before she had time to think of the consequences. 'No, I do not, as it happens!' she retorted. 'But if I loved him, then nothing you could say would stop me from wanting him—no matter how ''unsuitable'' a partner you might deem me to be!'

A wry smile brushed the corners of his hard mouth, a combination of admiration and relief, and Lucy realised that she had given him exactly the answer he wanted. She had made it clear that they were indeed just lovers—and that Guido had no desire nor intention to make their relationship anything more than that. Gianferro could now see that she presented no danger. No threat. No wonder all the tension had left his hard, lean body.

'Good,' he said quietly. 'I am glad that we understand each other.'

He rose to his feet, gesturing for her to follow suit, and Lucy found herself wondering fleetingly what it must be like always to orchestrate each and every situation. To decide when to stand, to sit, to talk or not to talk. Did the burden of it all become too much sometimes, even for him? Was that why his almost cruel mouth so rarely smiled?

'Yes, your Serene Highness,' she said calmly.

He nodded, as if in acknowledgement of her curtsey. 'There is a member of staff waiting outside to conduct you to the infant Prince now.'

She bobbed him another curtsey and left the room, to follow a silent servant down one of the long, wide corridors, feeling like a tiny tadpole who had just been thrown into shark-infested waters. Was this what went on behind the Palace doors, then? Behind-the-scenes wheeling and dealing?

It is what it is, she told herself—and someone like you isn't going to be able to change it.

Her troubled thoughts flew straight out of her head when she was ushered into the Palace Nursery. The sight which greeted her made her heart turn over with a wistful kind of longing.

She barely noticed Guido's younger brother, nor the tawny-haired woman who was standing beside him. All she could see was Guido—her *casual* lover, she thought with an unwelcome pang—cradling the baby in his arms.

There was always something sweet about men who were unused to babies having to deal with them— although 'sweet' wasn't a word which would automatically sit comfortably with a man as overtly masculine as Guido.

But sweet he looked. Whatever she had seen him do, it had always looked utterly effortless and accomplished, but as he tentatively held the infant she surprised a bleak, almost anguished look in his eyes. Was that a need for reassurance, perhaps? Because he was unused to holding such a precious bundle and needed to know that he was doing it properly?

The tawny-haired woman beamed at him. 'Why, Guido, you're doing just fine!' she exclaimed, in an accent which surprised Lucy as being not unlike her own. But then, Prince Nicolo had defied convention and married an English girl.

Lucy saw Guido tense before she moved forward. They all looked up, but everything seemed to melt away into the background, for all she was aware of was the ebony eyes which were dazzling her with their dark fire.

'It's Lucy,' Guido said, in a tone she didn't quite understand. 'Back from her cosy little chat with Gianferro!'

Was he angry that she had insisted on facing

Gianferro on her own? And was that less from a sense of wanting to protect her and more from the fact that he liked to be in control?

Putting her troubled thoughts aside, she smiled as she approached him. 'What a beautiful baby,' she said softly, and tentatively touched the delicate silk of his little dark head.

The woman might be a princess, but first and foremost she was a mother, and she beamed at Lucy with fierce maternal pride.

'Isn't he?' she cooed, her mouth breaking into an infectious smile as she held her hand out. 'And you must be Lucy. I'm Ella, and this is my husband, Nico.'

Nico—or Prince Nicolo Louis Fantone Cacciatore, to be more precise—was younger than Guido, but with the same lean, muscular body, black hair and dark, golden good looks. Both men were heart-stoppingly handsome, but Nico's face was softer than his brother's—and you could see a certain air of serenity as he looked at his wife and his son, an inner glow which only added to his masculinity instead of detracting from it.

That's love, thought Lucy—not lust. And a cloud passed over her heart.

'*Enchanté,*' he murmured, and raised Lucy's hand to his lips in a gesture which managed to be both courteous and gloriously old-fashioned at the same time. Then he turned to his brother, with mischief in his black eyes. 'A woman who is both brave as well as beautiful, no doubt?'

'Brave?' questioned Lucy, with a frown.

'You will have needed all the courage in the world to deal with my eldest brother,' teased Nico.

'How *was* Gianferro?' drawled Guido.

'Charming,' said Lucy diplomatically, and Ella shot her the briefest of sympathetic glances.

I bet she had to go through the same kind of interrogation with him, thought Lucy. But in her case it was warranted. She was in love with Nico, and he with her. Whereas in her case she was just here because…because…

Behind her fringe, her brow creased into a tiny frown. Just why *had* Guido brought her here? To keep his bed warm at night? Surely not. He had never seemed in need of close, intimate companionship in the past.

With an effort she pulled herself away from unanswerable thoughts and looked down at the sleeping bundle in Guido's arms, thinking what a contrast it made—the tiny baby cradled within his powerful grip.

'What's…what's his name?' she questioned.

'It's Leo,' answered Ella, and her wide mouth crinkled into a smile. 'Well, Leonardo Amadore Constantinus Cacciatore, actually—but Leo for short! Would you like to hold him?'

'Oh, I would! Can I?'

'Of course you can! That's if Guido can bear to let him go!' said Ella impishly.

'You like babies?' questioned Nico softly.

She looked up into a face which was so like Guido's yet a million miles away from his hard, handsome stare. 'I love them.' Lucy's voice was fervent, but then she had always been hands-on with her friends' children.

Guido's eyes narrowed. 'Here, Lucy.' His voice was a murmur. 'You'd better take him.'

It seemed almost too intimate as she took the child which Guido passed over to her with the care he might have employed if it had been handling a ticking time-bomb, and at first she held the child in a similarly over-exaggerated way. For a moment she was acutely aware that this was a Royal prince, perhaps the future King of Mardivino, since neither Guido nor Gianferro had shown any sign of producing an heir. All babies were precious, but this baby…

But those thoughts were forgotten the instant she smelt his particular baby smell and saw the easy warmth and trust of his innocent sleep. Instinctively she pulled him closer to her. With equal instinct the baby jerked his head, blindly searching for her breast, and Lucy blushed. Ella's peal of laughter quickly dispelled any embarrassment, but she looked up to meet the steely stare of Guido and her feeling of apprehension increased.

Was he wondering—as she was—what had happened to the independent sex-bomb of a girlfriend he had brought with him? It was true that she had played her sensual part back in the suite, but it seemed to displease him that she was now cradling his nephew and cooing and blushing like any normal woman.

But surely that was the whole point—that underneath it all she was just a normal woman with normal

desires? It was all very well in principle to tell
yourself that you were just going to have a wild and
passionate affair, without letting any constricting
emotion get in the way. But that was what women
did. It was the way they were made—programmed to
react in a certain way, especially when there were
babies around.

'Here, Lucy. I'll take him,' said Ella, holding her
arms out. 'I'd better feed him before we go down to
dinner. Gianferro may be a total walk-over where his
nephew is concerned, but I doubt he'd appreciate it
if I started breastfeeding my son at a State Banquet!'

State Banquet! Guido hadn't mentioned *that*!
Though when she stopped to think about it what had
she expected—all of them having dinner on trays,
clustered around a television set?

Lucy again looked at Guido, but this time he wasn't
even glancing in her direction. Instead, his gaze was
roving rather distractedly around the Nursery suite.
As if he was seeing it for the first time.

As if he was wondering what the hell he was doing
there.

When she went into dinner Lucy thanked her lucky
stars that she *had* let Guido buy her some suitable
clothes for this trip, because otherwise... Otherwise
she would have been left *looking* like an outsider,
instead of just feeling like one.

As it was, the sleek black sheath was perfect. Silk-
satin and cut on the bias, it seemed to have the magical properties of managing to emphasise all her good

bits and completely disguise the bits she wasn't so fond of. Consequently, her breasts looked lush and her waist a mere handspan of a thing, while the curve of her hips seemed both shapely yet slim. Oh, how different the world would look if all the women in it could dress in couture!

She had pinned her hair up—the way she sometimes did for work—its Titian colour a lustrous redbrown gleam and its stark lines adding to the impact of the beautifully simple dress.

She had seen Guido's eyes darken as they watched her, but even as part of her had thrilled in the light of his silent and sensual appropation there had been something about his stern countenance which had made her wary.

For there was something so distant about him tonight. And not just physical distance—the fact that he was sitting far away from her at the long table, which was awash with beautiful flower arrangements and laid with ornate crystal and china.

It was as if he were a helium balloon and someone had cut the string which bound him to earth—sending him soaring ever higher into this lavish aristocratic stratosphere in which he moved so easily. While she was the little girl left staring at a fast-retreating, bobbing dot, knowing that she would never get it back again.

Oh, do stop it, Lucy, she urged herself, and pull yourself together. Just because he isn't smiling across the table at you!

For a woman who hadn't been going to read anything into anything she was doing a pretty good job of it!

So she fixed a smile to her lips and accepted a glass of champagne, and laughed obediently at the aged but rather amusing Count on her right side. After a while her laughter grew relaxed and natural, and she chatted to some visiting Lord on her other side, who was obviously out to flirt for Britain! And it was easy to ignore the women who were vying outrageously for Guido's attention—like a pack of fancy-plumaged vultures who were circling an especially delectable morsel.

Guido watched her, wondering why things which seemed so perfectly simple had a habit of complicating themselves.

What had prompted his strange sense of unease and the fleeting pang of some long-forgotten pain when he had been holding the baby? Thoughts of his mother and her death? Or was it merely that bringing a woman made everything seem so different? *He* was being treated differently, as if having a partner made him seem more human and approachable.

But it wasn't like that! Lucy was here as his lover and his distraction—and not just for him. As his partner she would send out a powerful message to the conniving matrons of Mardivino who were always so intent on manufacturing introductions to their precious daughters!

Hadn't he always longed for a relationship with a woman who thought as a man did? Who enjoyed the good things, like sex and laughter, and didn't produce the whole gamut of female emotions which made life so impossibly dreary and tortuous?

Was that what was troubling him? The fact that she had started coming over all gooey-eyed when she saw Leo? Or that she'd started looking a little too much at home? The trouble was that you got an image of a woman in your head, and when she started acting outside that image it made you feel you didn't know her.

He stared across the table at her. She was giggling at something the Englishman was whispering to her. His mouth hardened.

That was the whole point, surely? That he didn't *really* know her—and neither did he want to. That was what killed the excitement—once you started getting into that trap of caring and sharing and analysing every last damned thing. Or rather, when *they* did. Guido had never met a woman he could spend time with, day in and day out, in that parlous state they called commitment.

Lucy turned her head to look at him then, and very deliberately he ran the tip of his tongue over his lips. He saw her eyes darken and waited to see what she would do next, and he felt a hot jerk of sensual frustration to see her coolly turn her head and continue to talk to the man beside her.

After that the evening became an ordeal to be endured. He could barely wait to get her alone again, and yet he knew he had to—and matters were made even more exasperating by the fact that she seemed to be taking her time over everything.

It seemed to take for ever until he could get near

her, and when he did he dipped his head to her ear. 'Shall we slip away now?' he suggested silkily.

Lucy looked at him askance, though inside she was simmering. Ever since they had visited the Nursery he had virtually ignored her—apart from the occasional studied sexual stare. And now, at the very first opportunity, he wanted to whisk her away to bed. He hadn't even asked her to dance!

'Why, that would look terribly rude, Guido!' she reprimanded him softly. 'What *are* you thinking of? The band have only just started playing and I've had at least three offers to dance!'

He'd bet she had! He didn't like the tone of her voice, and neither did he like what she was saying. Had a few hours in the Palace been enough to make her forget her place in it? 'I don't need advice from you on how to behave in my own home!' he snapped.

'Well, I think you do!' she retorted sweetly. Let him stew! Let him... 'Oh—*oh*,' she gasped, as he pulled her into his arms without warning, his hard body pressing against the pliant softness of hers. 'What the hell do you think you're doing?'

'What does it look like?' he questioned as he slid his hand over her back, possessive against the bare skin, his fingertips tracing tiny unseen circles on her flesh which set her shivering. 'I'm claiming the first dance.'

Claiming. It sounded territorial—let's face it, it *was* territorial. So why was she letting him stroke her like that? Was she powerless to resist him, or simply unwilling? Close call.

Her head tipped back as if it was too heavy for her neck, and she could feel his warm breath close to her skin. 'Guido,' she said weakly, 'you must stop this.'

'But I'm not doing anything,' he said, as he pressed his hard heat against her.

'You know exactly what you're doing,' she gasped softly. 'You're using the dance to seduce me.'

God, yes. He could smell the desire on her skin, and he breathed it in like a man who had been drowning. 'And you don't like it?'

She opened her eyes very wide then, aware that her breath was coming in short, frantic bursts—like someone who had been running in a long, long race. How on earth was it possible to feel overwhelming passion at the same time as the heavy, stone-like ache of her heart at the realisation that *this* was what he wanted from her. Probably *all* he wanted from her.

But he had tortured *her*, so now let him have a taste of his own medicine. 'Oh, I love it,' she whispered. 'But it's making me wish that no one else was around. So that you could slide my expensive dress up...'

'And...and why would I want to do that?' he questioned shakily.

'To find out whether or not I was wearing any knickers, of course.'

'Aren't you?' he groaned.

'Well, yes—I am, actually. But we could soon dispose of those, couldn't we?' Fractionally, she pushed her breasts against him, and now it was his turn to moan. 'And then you could lift me up, wrap my legs

around your waist, and we could do it here...here...
right here and right now, Guido. Because that's what
you'd like, isn't it?'

He closed his eyes, because now the hot jerk of
desire was threatening to render him incapable of doing anything—except maybe acting out her outrageous fantasy. 'Can you feel what you've done to
me?' he bit out.

Could she? Lucy swallowed. 'Er, yes.'

'So how the hell am I going to get off this dance
floor.'

'You think of something so abhorrent that it completely freaks you out and makes you lose all that
desire in an instant.'

There was a long pause. Oh, that was easy! He
thought of marriage, and suddenly he was right back
where he wanted to be. In control.

Lucy stared at him, aware that the black eyes had
grown icy, and suddenly she was furious with herself.
Why had she played that stupid game with him?

'Guido?' she questioned, and uncharacteristically
her voice sounded weak and uncertain.

The smile he gave her was anticipatory, almost
cruel. He was enjoying the sensation now that the
situation was reversed and *she* was the one left doing
the wanting.

'I'll leave you to your dancing, Lucy,' he said
softly. 'Let me know when you want to go to bed.'

And something in his eyes made her feel
unaccountably scared.

CHAPTER SIX

THE following day, resplendent in a close-fitting jade-green suit, with a huge black picture hat trimmed with feathers, Lucy stood in Solajoya's small but majestic cathedral as Leo was baptised. The music of the organ and the accompanying choir soared celestially up to the high domed ceiling, and the church was filled with the great and the good of Mardivino as well as immediate family. Only the King was unable to attend—his health was too frail and these days, according to Guido, he rarely left his suite of rooms at the Palace.

Yet, despite the splendour and the grandeur, it was essentially a family occasion. Just as with every other family on the planet, there were small swapped smiles when Leo began to bawl as the water was sprinkled onto his forehead.

It was only when they stepped outside into blinding sunlight, where banks of fragrant flowers were massed, to the sound of cheers and the sight of what seemed to be the entire population of the island, that Lucy realised that it was a significant and very regal occasion, too.

Lunch was at the Palace—and far less formal than the State Banquet of the night before. This time Lucy was seated next to a woman named Sasha—a beauty not much older than herself, whose olive skin and dark eyes marked her out as a native of the island. She was sweet and charming, and incredibly interested to know all about Lucy.

'I can't believe that Guido has actually brought a woman home,' she confided softly.

Lucy smiled, though it felt brittle and unnatural.

When eventually they had gone back to their room last night, they had circled each other like two warring creatures. She had been wary of him, confused by him, and had wanted to distance herself from him—as he had done from her. To try to show him—and prove to herself—that he did not have an irresistible power over her.

How typical that her very reticence had seemed to entrance him and he had pulled out all the stops where charm was concerned. He had stroked her hair and told her that she was beautiful. Had undressed her slowly…oh, so slowly…as if he'd had all the time in the world.

Who could have resisted such advances, as he cajoled and soothed and incited her, all at the same time?

Even though a part of her had tried to fight it she had been unable to do so. He had made her molten and receptive and aching for him, as she always ached for him, and then they had fallen into bed and spent almost the whole night making love. Though maybe that was just her slant on what they had done.

The trouble was that there didn't seem to be any description which fell in between 'making love' and 'having sex'. It certainly hadn't been the former—

certainly not where Guido was concerned—and the latter sounded so...so clinical. And, whatever else it might have been, it had certainly not been clinical. It had been heavenly. Heartstopping. And once her turbulent emotions had melted under the onslaught of his caresses Lucy had had to bite back words of endearment.

Oh, why had she become involved with a man as unobtainable as Guido Cacciatore? And why had she not had the insight to realise that compartmentalising her feelings for him was as useless as whistling in the wind?

'So where did you two meet?' queried Sasha, with a smile.

'At a party.' Sasha's eyebrows were still raised in question. Lucy took another mouthful of champagne. 'In New York.'

'He loves New York,' said Sasha thoughtfully. 'But of course, it's where he went to live with his aunt, when his mother died.'

'I...I didn't know.'

Sasha shrugged. 'Well, you of all people know how closed-in he can be.'

She certainly did. 'Have you known him long?'

'Oh, all my life.' Sasha smiled again. 'Believe me, I've seen Guido in *all* his guises. We used to play together as children. He's a bit like...' She frowned, creasing up her nose. 'Not a brother, exactly—we're not close enough for that. More like a cousin—once or twice removed, I guess!'

Lucy hadn't thought he *was* particularly close to

his brothers, but she didn't say anything—and besides, she knew that the subtext to what Sasha was saying was that there was no romance—or longed-for romance—between her and Guido. Her reassurance was oddly comforting, and Lucy smiled.

'And you're a definite improvement on the last woman I saw him with!' said Sasha fervently.

It was one of those situations that you read about in women's magazines—where you knew you ought to completely ignore the statement and carry on talking about something else. But she couldn't help herself.

'Oh?' questioned Lucy casually. 'Who was that?'

'Oh, you know.' Sasha pulled a face. 'One of those sooty-eyed blondes who look like they're composed of plastic and silicone!'

In spite of herself, Lucy laughed. She wasn't naïve enough to think that Guido had come to her bed as a virgin! 'When was that?'

'Oh…ages ago. Last fall, I think. Yes. I'd flown to New England, and then called in to see Guido on the way back here.'

The sounds of chatter retreated and were replaced by a sudden roaring in her ears. Lucy's mouth dried and she quickly drank some more champagne, which made it even drier. She was aware that a pulse was slamming somewhere in her temple, as if someone was repeatedly knocking a hammer hard against it.

Last fall? Autumn?

So when would that have been?

September, maybe? Or even October?

But she had started her affair with him in June!

She felt the bitter taste of betrayal which made the champagne a distant memory. Had he been…oh, that horrible phrase…*two-timing* her?

How she kept her face from reacting she never knew. Maybe she had become an expert through hiding her real feelings from Guido. But whatever it was, she just managed a cool, grown-up smile. After all, there could be any kind of explanation…wasn't that what always happened in books? That the sooty-eyed blonde was really his sister?

But he didn't have a sister!

His cousin?

She kept the cool smile pinned to her lips. She would not jump to conclusions. Nor would she put Sasha in an uncomfortable position. She would ask him herself. Later.

And then, disturbing her thoughts with the rippling precision of a flat, round pebble thrown into an already turbulent pool, she heard his deep, dark accent.

'Are you having a good time, *cara mia*?' he murmured.

She turned her head to look up at him, grateful for the large hat which shaded her face and the troubled look in her eyes. He was wearing a suit and a snowy shirt, and a silken tie as sapphire as the blue waters of the sea which could be seen quite clearly through the Palace windows.

Last night he had been edgy, almost irritable, but it was amazing what a night of brilliant sex could do—for today he was as sunny as it was possible for a man like Guido to be. His black eyes were glittering with life and fire, and his olive skin gleamed with a kind of soft inner luminescence. He looked vibrant and vital and thoroughly irresistible, and her pulse began to scramble in a thin and thready way.

'It's lovely,' she said quietly, because in a way it was. If you had shown someone a photograph of the scene, they would have longed to be there themselves. The baby was now sleeping, and there was the smooth and easy flow of chatter which came at the end of a very agreeable gathering. 'Quite lovely,' she repeated, looking around as if she wanted to freeze-frame the scene, to lock it away in her mind so that she would never forget it.

Guido's eyes narrowed. There was something in her expression which he couldn't quite read, and he thought—not for the first time—what an enigmatic person she really was. She seemed to buck the modern trend of spilling her innermost feelings and thoughts within a nanosecond of knowing someone— and wasn't there something both intriguing and devastatingly appealing about a woman who always kept something back?

He bent his head even closer, so that his words were murmured enticements in her ear. 'Things will be breaking up here soon. What do you say to going back to our room—for a siesta? Mmm?'

Lucy swallowed. She would bet that his idea of a siesta didn't fit the traditional definition, but in a way wasn't that exactly what she needed? Not the physical part—which was doubtless his reason for asking her—but the opportunity to ask him about the blonde, and to ask him something else, too…

She smiled. 'Only if you're sure your brother and sister-in-law won't think we are rude to leave.'

'Are you crazy?' He raised his eyebrows. 'My brother would consider me lacking in any kind of sanity to do otherwise. Come.'

Quietly, they slipped away, and Lucy felt almost light-headed as they stole through the cool marble corridors. For this was all a farce—this pretence that no one knew where they were going, or guessed what their—his—intention was. The other guests would notice their absence, but it was more than that—there were servants along the way—always servants. Sometimes, like now, knowing they were not wanted, they would melt away—as if they were not composed of flesh and blood at all.

Yet Lucy knew that if Guido had the slightest wish or desire—for a drink, say, or a newspaper or book—then those self-same faceless servants would magically interpret what he wanted and would appear discreetly by his side to do his bidding.

Did that kind of attention all your life change you? It must do. When you became used to having a small world revolve around you then surely you could be forgiven for thinking that the normal rules of restraint and fidelity did not apply.

Did they?

Well, she was soon going to find out.

Once they were back in their suite, he carefully took her hat off and then, with equal care, unpinned her hair so that it spilled down over the green jacket of her suit. *The suit that he'd bought for her.* If you allowed a man to buy you clothes, then weren't you selling something of yourself into the bargain?

'Did I tell you how beautiful you looked today?' he murmured, stroking at the tip of her chin and then lifting it slightly with his fingertips, as if wanting to examine her face more closely.

She had planned not to let him touch her, but oh, how seductive a gentle, almost protective touch could be. Perhaps if he had gone all out for a blatant and hot-blooded seduction then she might not have been so responsive. As it was, all her nerve-endings seemed acutely sensitised, as if her skin was raw and new, craving the healing of his caress.

Should she let him continue? she thought wildly. Pretend that there were not questions bubbling away at the back of her mind and give herself up to his embrace and everything that would follow? Knowing deep down that it might be the last chance she could do so? One last taste of enchanted food before she went back to more normal fare?

But no. Passion was strong, but pride could be even more powerful. She pulled away from him and went to stare out of the window instead.

Outside, the soft breeze made the petals of the fragrant roses shimmer like a heat-haze. There were pink and gold and crimson flowers, and softest apricot, too. And a mass of white blooms surrounding a statue— looking as pure and as perfect as the clouds which scudded across the azure sky.

Who would have thought that an ordinary girl like her could end up somewhere like this? In a Palace. With a devastatingly handsome prince standing in the room behind her, desperate to take her clothes off and take her into his bed once more.

Sweet dreams are made of this, she thought—but inside, as relentless as the beating of her heart, was the awareness that the dream was in danger of turning sour.

She turned round and found his dark eyes narrowed, watchful—but then, Guido was a very perceptive man. He had sensed that something was not right but, like a consummate poker player, he was biding his time—waiting for her to play her hand before he came back with something to trump her. And could he? Were her misgivings and her unvoiced fears completely groundless? She prayed they were, conscious of the lack of conviction of her hopes.

But her question, when it came, was not the one she had been planning to ask. It was almost as if she was seeking background knowledge for the question which would follow. Like someone doing research into motive.

'Why did you bring me here with you, Guido?'

'You know why. I thought you would enjoy it.' He frowned. 'I thought you *were* enjoying it. Aren't you?'

She didn't answer that. 'Is it just because of that? I mean—there is no ulterior motive?'

There was a pause. She was not only an independent woman, but an intelligent one, too. Would it insult that intelligence if he tried to convince her that a dip into Royal life in the luxurious surroundings of Mardivino had been his only objective?

The question was whether she was grown-up enough to accept him as the man he really was—with all his faults as well as the qualities of any other man.

He shrugged his shoulders and accompanied the very Gallic gesture with a rueful smile. 'It is useful, having you here,' he murmured.

Of all the most insulting words he could have used, Lucy would have put *useful* in the top five. But what exactly did he mean? 'Useful?' she echoed, perplexed.

He began to loosen his tie. Could he make her understand? 'My presence here always invites a kind of feeding frenzy.'

'Feeding frenzy?' she echoed again, feeling like someone who was learning a new language by the simple repetition of a phrase. 'What do you mean?'

'I mean that the inhabitants of this island seem to feel it necessary to marry off their Princes; there is pressure on Gianferro to do so, but particularly on me. Gianferro's bride will be cherry-picked from a very small and exclusive orchard, but the field is rather wider in my case. Especially now that Nico, the youngest, has settled down and provided Mardivino with a new generation.'

He had the grace to look slightly abashed as he stared at her, looking almost little-boy-lost with those melting dark eyes. Did he think that such grace would absolve him from what he had revealed? Or that by being allowed to see a glimpse of vulnerability she would forgive him anything?

'Let me get this straight,' she said, and her voice didn't sound anything like her usual voice. 'My invitation—apart from giving you the obvious benefits of having a willing sexual partner who would place no demands on you—was a kind of talisman—or maybe woman—' she gave an ironic laugh '—who would ward off any prospective brides?'

'That's too simplistic a way of looking at it!' he protested.

'Is it?' She noticed that he didn't deny it—but how could he, when basically what she'd said was true? And would he answer the next question—the ramifications of which might really sound the death-knell to their relationship? But she reminded herself that the word *relationship* had a hollow ring about it in their case. What they had was not that at all—it was something merely masquerading as a partnership.

Her eyes were very clear, but her voice sounded strained as the words came tumbling out. 'Did you happen to go to bed with a blonde last September?'

He stilled in the process of pulling his tie off and his eyes narrowed into shards of smoky ebony. *'What?'* he questioned softly.

'You didn't hear me? Or you didn't understand?' she demanded, but pain had started to rip through her at the glaring omission of a denial. 'It's a simple enough question, Guido—all it requires is a simple yes or no answer. Did you or did you not sleep with a blonde woman last fall?'

'How dare you interrogate me in this way?'

'Is that a yes?' she asked steadily. 'Or a no?'

They stared at each other across a space which seemed to be enlarging by the second.

He nodded his head. 'Well, yes,' he said. 'But it meant—'

'Nothing?' she supplied sarcastically, and now the tear in her heart was widening, and someone was tipping into the space a substance with all the painful and abrasive qualities of grit. 'Isn't that what men always say? That it didn't mean anything? So not only do they damn the woman they betrayed, but also the woman they betrayed her with!'

'*Betrayed?*' he exploded. 'Do not use such emotive words with me, Lucy! I had met you on precisely two occasions up until that moment!'

'But you had slept with *me*!' she whimpered, like a dog whose master was raising the whip.

'So? For God's sake—don't you think you're over-reacting?'

She felt sick. 'How is that?' She trembled. 'How am I overreacting?'

'Because at the time what we had was casual. It was new. It was uncertain. It was all those things which are true at the beginning, and sometimes the beginning is the end.'

'Don't try to confuse me with your warped logic!' she raged.

'I am trying to tell it like it is,' he said, with a forced patience which was unfamiliar territory to him.

'We had made no arrangement to see one another again, had we? Remember?'

Through the mists of her pain she looked back through her memory, blindly searching for something which would make it all acceptable. The mists cleared. She had been back-to-back on a series of long-haul flights which had clashed with his trips around the globe in exactly the opposite direction. And, yes, in theory he was right—they had *not* made any arrangement to see one another again.

In fact, he had told her casually to ring him, but she had not bothered. She had been in that early stage of a relationship where she was uncertain of him—not sure whether he really wanted to see her again and not wanting to pursue *him* because that way lay heartbreak and the loss of respect.

Lucy had recognised that for a man like Guido the chase was everything, and that once a woman started reversing the traditional role she would be doomed.

She had almost been over him when his call had come, out of the blue.

'I thought you were going to call me!' he had accused softly.

'I've been busy,' she'd retorted.

'Oh, have you?' He had laughed, and his voice had dipped into a honeyed caress. He had been trying to forget her. She had touched him in a way he was not familiar with—a way which spelt some unknown danger and not the kind he wanted to embrace. But it had not worked. He had not forgotten her at all. 'I've missed you, Lucy,' he'd murmured, and she had been lost.

Intellectually, she could see now the logic behind his reasoning—but jealousy was a different plant altogether, and it flourished and grew like a weed.

'And how many more?' she demanded hotly. 'How many since?'

'None!' he exploded. 'After that it was only you— you know it was!'

On some level, yes, she did—for their lovemaking had been completely different when they had met up again. It was as if the break had allowed the barriers between them to fall—certainly the sexual ones. She had felt freer and more liberated—able to indulge his fantasies. And her own.

Perhaps she could have forgiven him then, had it not been for his motive for bringing her here. Her secret little dreams, that he'd wanted to introduce her to his family and to deepen their relationship, had been as nebulous as dreams always were.

'It still doesn't change your reasons for bringing me here.' She stared at him sadly. 'Have I reached such elevated heights in your regard for me that I should rejoice that you've brought me here to see off other women? To protect you from their advances like a human guard-dog?'

'You are making a....' For the first and only time since she had known him he seemed to struggle to find the right words in English. 'A mountain out of the molehill!' he declared passionately.

But then something snapped, and her own temper

exploded to match his. 'I don't think so!' she raged. 'I think that nothing very much has changed at all, if you must know! It was casual way back then, and it is still casual now!' Hadn't she said as much to Gianferro yesterday?

There was a fraught and odd kind of pause, which could never have been described as silence—for the sound of their breathing punctured the air with accusations and hurt.

'So what do you want to do about it?' he said eventually. 'Are you going to shout and rage a little more and then come over here and let me kiss it better?'

As if it was a tiny graze on her knee instead of a jagged, deep tear through her heart! She closed her eyes briefly to blink away the salty glimmer of tears, then shook her head. 'No. I want to go home,' she said shakily. 'And then I never want to see you again.'

He stared at her, scarcely able to believe what she was saying. 'Don't play games with me, Lucy,' he warned softly. 'For I have no appetite for them. If you threaten to leave then I will arrange it. But I shall not run after you, nor plead with you to stay. That is not my style.'

No, she couldn't imagine that it was. But she was not playing games—she was deadly serious.

'Then arrange it. Please.'

His narrowed eyes raked over her one last time. 'So be it,' he ground out, like a skater digging his blade repeatedly into the ice. He turned on his heel and slammed his way out of the suite, leaving Lucy looking after him, biting her lip to stop herself from crying.

Yet even while she was silently damning herself for ever having asked him anything the one subject she had not broached loomed up like a dark spectre in her mind.

But it was easy to flatten it down again.

Her philosophy on life had developed largely because her job involved a great deal of flying. Accidents *did* happen occasionally, but there was absolutely no point in worrying about them until they did.

CHAPTER SEVEN

HE COULD be a prince and you could be an air stewardess, but it made no difference—at the end of the day you were still both just a man and a woman, with all the problems that men and women had when they began relationships. Or—in her and Guido's case—ended them.

And what a problem it was.

Lucy stared at the blue line, as if looking at it long enough and hard enough might somehow change the end result. Her sense of disbelief was tempered by the hysteria which was growing by the moment.

She had gone through anger, concern, outright worry, denial, and now—now the most terrifying thing of all…

Confirmation.

She swallowed, putting the palm of her hand over her still-flat belly as if trying to convince herself that it wasn't true, that she couldn't be pregnant.

Could she?

She heard muffled moving around coming from the direction of the sitting room and her head jerked up. Gary was home! So what did she do? Did she tell him?

There was a loud banging on the bathroom door.

'You in there, Luce?'

She licked her lips nervously. 'Yes.'

'Well, are you going to be all day? I've got a hot date tonight and I need to beautify myself!'

Normally she would have giggled and vacated the bathroom while he had her in stitches about his love-life. Gary was a fellow steward, sweet and handsome and understanding and gay—and he seemed to spend ten times as long in the bathroom as Lucy did.

She had never felt less like giggling in her life. But she couldn't hide away in here for ever, and if she didn't tell someone soon she was going to be sick.

You already *have* been sick, she reminded herself. Long and retchingly this very morning, and yesterday morning, and for countless mornings before that.

She pulled open the door and was shocked to see the look of horror on Gary's good-looking face.

'What the hell is wrong?' he demanded.

How to tell him? How to tell anyone when she'd only just been able to bear accepting it for herself?

'I'm…I'm…'

His eyes raked around the floor of their usually immaculate bathroom. 'Oh, my God—you're pregnant!' he yelped.

'How…how could you tell?' Did that mean she actually *looked* pregnant?

He pursed his lips and his eyes flicked to the discarded cardboard box and the plastic strip which was lying in the sink. 'This may not be quite my scene—but you wouldn't need to be a detective to work it out. How long ago and who…?' The look of horror came over his face once again, and momentarily he clapped his hand over his mouth. 'Oh, God—don't tell me—it's the Prince!'

'Of course it's the Prince!' said Lucy tearfully. 'Who else do you think it could be? And his name is Guido.' Somehow that made it sound and seem more real. She couldn't possibly be pregnant by a prince, but she could be pregnant by a man with a real name—even if it was an exotically foreign one.

'Oh, love,' said Gary sympathetically, and gave her shoulder a squeeze. 'What on earth are you going to do?'

Tears welled up in her eyes and she scrubbed at them furiously with her fist. 'I'm going to have to tell him.'

Lucy.

The name flashed up on the screen of his mobile and Guido glanced at it with unflickering eyes, tempted to ignore it.

Why? Because that little ember of anger still smouldered away inside him? Anger that she—*she*—had had the temerity to leave him, when no woman had ever done so before? Or was it because she had made him feel bad about himself, and Guido didn't like to feel bad? He liked to float through life, taking only the good bits and discarding anything which looked as if it would even remotely lead to complications.

But even his anger could not quite extinguish his interest.

Why was she ringing him after having told him that

she never wanted to set eyes on him again? Was she maybe regretting her words and her actions? Remembering, perhaps, how good they were together...wanting a little more?

Even while desire leapt inside him, he half hoped that was not so. For Guido respected Lucy, and her adamant stance and her pride, and for him that kind of respect was rare—almost unheard of. Obviously she wanted more from a man than he was capable of giving—or wanted to give—and in a funny kind of way he respected that, too.

If she came back then surely his esteem for her would die. She would become like all the others, who would sacrifice their principles for a man who might never be King but would always be Prince...

Curiosity got the better of him, and he flicked the button with his thumb.

'*Si?*' he drawled.

'It's Lucy.'

'I know it is,' he said softly.

Then why the hell didn't you say, Hello, Lucy? She hesitated, because she couldn't think how to say it—and even if she could was it fair to blurt it out over the phone?

'How are you?' he questioned, because now he was perplexed. Had he been expecting one of those predictable conversations? The ones where the woman brightly asked how he was, and acted as if no harsh words had been spoken, and then casually mentioned that they just happened to be passing through...

It was a question she could not answer truthfully. 'I have to see you.'

Guido stared at the gleaming skyline and raised his dark eyebrows by a fraction. So she had come straight out with her desire to see him. Pretty up-front—if a little surprising. And yet there was no longing in her voice, no sultry undertone saying that she had missed him. The unpredictable was rare enough to excite him.

'Where are you?'

'In England.'

He frowned. 'And when are you coming to New York?'

'I'm not.'

'Then…?'

She drew a deep breath as she heard his faint puzzlement—as if to say, *Well, why are you ringing me, then?*

'I'm at home, in England.'

Pull yourself together, Lucy. But what could she say? *Come and visit me here because I can't face travelling?* He might refuse, and then where would that leave her? Which left her absolutely no choice at all but to tell him.

'Guido, I'm pregnant.'

He felt as he had never felt in his life—as if a dark whirlwind had swirled its way into his lungs, pushing all the natural breath away. For a moment he could not speak.

'What did you say?' he questioned at last, softly and dangerously.

She was not going to be cast in the role of the baddie, the guilty party. There were two people involved here, and they must both share the consequences—whatever they might be.

'You heard.'

'It's mine?'

She bit down on her lip. She was not going to cry. 'Yes.'

'You're sure?'

'Sure that I'm pregnant, you mean? Or sure that it's yours? Yes, on both counts.'

Guido's words were like bitter stones spitting from his mouth. 'What is your address?'

He didn't even know where she lived! With a feeling of hysteria she told him, aware of the almost laughable contrast between his penthouse apartment or his Rainbow Palace. 'Number five Western Road, Brentwood.'

'I'll be there tomorrow,' he said tightly, and terminated the connection.

Unable to concentrate, and fired up by the need to fill her waking moments with any kind of activity which might temporarily give her the comfort of allowing her to forget her precarious situation, Lucy cleaned the house from top to bottom.

Gary stood in the doorway, watching her scrub the floor on her hands and knees. 'What's this?' he questioned. 'Penance?'

'I want the place to look clean,' she said stubbornly. 'It might be an ordinary little suburban house, but it will gleam as brightly as any damned Rainbow Palace!'

'We do have a mop, you know,' he said mildly.

Lucy's mouth wobbled into a smile. 'I'm treating it as a mini-workout!'

Gary breathed a sigh of relief. 'Thank God you're smiling again!'

'Being miserable isn't going to change anything.'

'That's my gal! What time is he arriving?'

'He didn't say. This afternoon, probably.'

'Just my luck to be flying off to Singapore in a minute!' Gary put his hand on his hip in an overtly camp gesture which made her smile again. 'You know I'd always wanted to meet a real-live prince!'

By mid-afternoon the house was gleaming—and there were fresh flowers in vases and the smell of furniture polish wafting in the air. Why didn't she go the whole hog and bake a cake while she was at it? *Because you aren't selling your house, that's why. And neither are you selling yourself.*

She didn't know what she was going to say to him, but she knew that she was not going to allow him to talk her into anything she didn't want. And—

The doorbell rang and Lucy froze. She shut her eyes briefly. How many times in your life did you wish that something was just a bad dream?

Guido glanced down the road as he waited for her to answer. He had never been anywhere like this in his life—it was like a parallel universe. Neat little semi-detached houses, with sparkling windows and tidy gardens. He could hear the sound of birds, and walking down the road towards him was a woman with a pushchair, and a chubby toddler by her side, who kept stopping to peer at the pavement. He stared hard at them in a way he would never normally have done, and his mouth tightened as the door opened and there stood Lucy.

For a moment he was taken aback to see that she looked just the same—slim and strong and curvy. Had he somehow expected her to be already swollen? Perhaps wearing some floaty smock thing to disguise a growing bump? His eyes narrowed. No, not the same at all—there were faint shadows beneath her honey-coloured eyes and her face was pale. The world seemed suddenly silent—an immense, important silence—and yet his words, when they came, were ordinary words.

'Hello, Lucy.'

Just the sight of him made her heart turn over, as she had suspected it would anyway. But her feelings for Guido were deeper and more complex now—for this was the man who had sired the child which grew inside her. A strong and powerful man. How she yearned to just let him take over and protect her—an instinct which perhaps went hand-in-hand with pregnancy itself. But he was offering to do neither, and she did not have the right to ask—she had relinquished all such rights the day she had walked out on him…

Her heart was racing—could that be good for the baby?—and she nodded in acknowledgement. 'You'd better come in.'

It was a bit like stepping into a larger version of a dolls' house he had once seen as a child in a museum, when he had been staying with his aunt. He'd had no idea that proportions could be so scaled-down—that rooms could be so small!

She led the way into a yellow and white sitting room, and he was surprised by the sudden understanding of a word which was not usually in his vocabulary. *Cosy.*

'Would you like some coffee?'

He shook his head. 'No, I do not want coffee.' And then, because they both seemed in danger of ignoring something in the hope that it might just go away, he said, 'How many weeks?'

'I'm not sure—'

'How can you not be sure?' he demanded.

'We can work it out,' she said desperately.

'You haven't been to see the doctor?'

'Not yet.'

She saw the anger and the disbelief which sparked flames in the coal-dark eyes, and yet with a blinding blow of surprise she realised that not once had he interrogated her about who the father was. Which meant he believed her. A relief she hadn't been anticipating washed over her and she felt compelled to offer some kind of explanation. 'I was…in denial, I guess.'

'You did not plan it?' he questioned coldly.

A wave of dizziness swept over her. 'Plan it? You think I planned it? What? To try to trap you or something? Well, think again, Guido, that isn't my style—

and even if it were there were two of us. It isn't just the woman who is responsible for contraception—it's the man's responsibility, too!'

Something unfamiliar stole over him. A sense that here was something which he couldn't just have someone solve for him by snapping his fingers.

'Sit down,' he ordered quietly.

Maybe if she hadn't been feeling so woozy and so perilously close to tears she might have told him that she didn't need permission to sit down in her own home. As it was, she collapsed in one of the armchairs as if her knees had been turned into gelatine.

His eyes narrowed as he did a swift mental calculation. 'I remember when it was,' he said slowly.

He had been showing her round the Palace and she had made him laugh, made him feel...*normal* in those formal surroundings, and something primitive had ripped through him. Something so primitive that he had neglected to protect himself and her—and when before in his life had *that* happened?

There had been an overwhelming need to take her swiftly and without ceremony—a truly novel experience for a man whose upbringing had been swamped with ceremony. No, she was right. It *had* been his responsibility, too—and passion had made it fly straight out of his head. Damn the witch! He had recognised that for him she spelt danger, and it seemed that he had been right.

His eyes sparked with black fire, but what good would anger do him now? He needed his wits about him to achieve what he needed to achieve.

'Nearly three months, I make it,' he said.

Some of her strength began to return as she heard the clipped note in his voice, and her eyes flashed defiance at him. 'I'm having the baby!' she declared. 'No matter what you say!'

He registered this, his mind sifting through all the possibilities. He was left with the same and only one which had occupied his mind all during the flight. The question was how he should go about achieving it—for he knew that beneath today's rather shaky Lucy lay a woman with steely resolve. Who could walk out of his door without turning back.

'I agree,' he murmured.

She was in such turmoil that it didn't even occur to her to tell him that she didn't actually *need* his consent. Instead, she looked at him with suspicion. 'You want me to keep the baby?'

He flinched as if she had struck him. 'Did you imagine that I would contemplate any alternative?' he questioned, in a low, shocked voice.

For a moment she felt like a drowning woman who had been offered not just a lifeline but a warm change of clothes at the end of it. And then he snatched them all away with his next words.

'Have you not considered that you carry within you a child of noble blood?'

'Every baby—any baby—is noble in my view!' she declared.

A faint smile curved the cruel lips. 'I commend you for your passion, Lucy,' he said softly. 'But I am looking at this from a purely practical point of view.'

The black eyes bored into her, as coolly analytical as a lawyer's eyes might have been. 'You are carrying my child—a child in whose veins beats the Royal blood of Mardivino.'

Now who was being passionate? she thought tiredly.

'By birth, that child will have certain rights and privileges. He or she could one day become King or Queen if Gianferro does not produce an heir—which looks increasingly likely.'

No, Lucy had been wrong. It had *not* been passion she had heard in his voice—it had been practicality. Now he was discussing their child's position in Mardivinian society as a conquering army might discuss dividing up the spoils of a country.

She rubbed her fingers over her forehead. 'I don't know what you think we can do about it. If anything. We aren't a couple any more.' She gave a short laugh. 'If indeed we ever were.'

He stared at her. Was she mad? Did she think he was just going to accept her momentous piece of news and walk away from her? Allow her to bring up his child—a Mardivinian Prince or Princess—in this little house in the middle of suburban England?

Like a chess master edging towards a win, he considered his next move with care. The burning question was whether the baby was indeed his. He looked down into her pale and beautiful face. The faint tremble of her bare lips unexpectedly stabbed at his conscience and as he gazed into the honey-coloured eyes the burning pride and dignity he read there left him in no doubt. And doubt, he recognised with an over-whelming certainty, would be the one thing guaran-teed to thwart his wishes. Her baby was his.

He felt the rapid acceleration of his heart, accom-panied by an almost dizzy feeling and a strange, blunted pain where his heart should be—if every woman he'd ever known hadn't accused him of not having one. He shook his head, shaken by the unfa-miliar physical sensations and the random process of his thoughts.

He was in shock!

But now was not the time to examine his reaction to impending fatherhood—there were matters far more urgent and pressing.

'The child must be born on Mardivino,' he said quietly.

'Must?' She stared at him.

'Do not fight me on this, Lucy,' he warned.

'But you don't live there!' she protested. 'You left your Royal life behind a long time ago—remember? You told me!'

'So I did.' His mouth hardened. 'But things are different now.'

How was it that he had slipped so quickly back into a traditional outlook? As if all those years of freedom had not happened. For a moment he felt dazed by the realisation of how indelibly his birthright had stamped its mark on him.

She tried one last attempt, knowing that she was fighting against something, but not quite sure what it was. 'It doesn't have to be difficult, Guido. Lots of women manage on their own—we can work something out.'

But he cut across her opposition as if it was of no consequence. 'Not only must the birth take place within the Principality,' he continued, 'it must also be legitimised.'

Her head was spinning now. 'What are you talking about?'

'Your Prince has come, *cara*,' he drawled sardonically. 'And he intends to marry you.'

Marry her? With a shotgun held to his back? 'No!'

'Oh, yes,' he said, and even though it was silky soft, there was no mistaking the undercurrent of steely purpose. 'You may wish to play the courageous single mother, but the reality will be an entirely different matter. It isn't going to happen. My baby will not be born illegitimately—he or she will inherit all that is their due, but that can only be achieved within wedlock.'

She stared at him, frozen into immobility by the iron edge of his words and the realisation that she had never seen Guido like this before. So cold and so powerful, and so...determined.

'Guido—'

'Don't even think of fighting me on this one, Lucy,' he said harshly. 'The odds are stacked highly enough in my favour to make it a laughably one-sided battle.' There was a pause to drive home his words, as if one was needed. 'Which I would win.'

She looked into his eyes and knew that he meant

it. Which meant that Lucy Maguire was going to marry a Prince.

It should have been a dream come true—but the reality was something different. It meant being shackled to a sexy but cold-blooded aristocrat. A man who didn't love her.

No, it was not a dream.

It was a living nightmare.

CHAPTER EIGHT

THEY were to be married quietly on Mardivino, on this blustery autumn day, with only their immediate families in attendance—including Lucy's rather bewildered parents, who kept looking around them as if expecting to wake up at any second. You and me both, she thought, rather grimly.

Her brother was a different matter, taking the whole bizarre situation in his stride and joking to her that she'd done 'better than I could ever have imagined, sis!' As if she'd won the Lottery!

But she knew that Benedict meant what he said. And that he actually liked Guido and thought he was a good man.

Well, of course he did! Hadn't Guido gone out of his way to win him round? Taking him sailing around the island and introducing him to glamorous women, and laying on bucketfuls of charm—which would have had even the most hardened cynic eating out of his hand?

Come to think of it he had been equally persuasive in winning Lucy over, getting her to agree to marry him—but in her case he had certainly not used charm. She wondered that he had not even bothered to try.

Perhaps he'd had no stomach for it, or perhaps he had instinctively realised that she would shrink away from it. For charm was nothing but a superficial and shallow veneer which people used as a front to hide their true feelings.

Instead, he had argued with cold and remorseless logic, citing historic precedent, making her dizzy with facts about the Mardivinian royal family and its progeny.

She supposed that if anything could be said in his favour it was that he hadn't bothered to dress up their proposed marriage to be something it wasn't.

And in the end she had been too tired to fight him, recognising that the full weight of a powerful regime would swing behind him if she dared to oppose his wishes. But perhaps pregnancy made you more vulnerable and susceptible—for she had found herself unable to let her own self-interest deny her baby its rights. What woman in her right mind would?

It would, he told her, be first and foremost a legal contract between them—and anything which went beyond that would have to be negotiated between them.

Their lawyers had thrashed out a long-prenuptial agreement. Lucy had engaged the best lawyer she could afford and she had taken his advice—though she had argued in vain about the clause which stated that should they divorce then the Cacciatore family would get custody of her child.

'Can they do that?' she had asked heatedly.

The lawyer had given a rather thin smile. 'Oh, yes. No contest—though you could try. Though can you see the courts letting you put a royal child with minders—while you carry on flying? These people will get whatever it is they want, make no mistake.'

So that was the deal. If she wanted to keep her child then she must stay married to its father.

And now here she was, on her way to the ceremony in all her bridal finery, with her stomach tied up in knots and feeling none of the joyful expectation of the normal bride.

'Good heavens,' breathed her father faintly as their horsedrawn carriage came to a halt in front of the cathedral steps. 'Just look at all those people!'

There were hordes of them—all waving flags and clutching flowers and cheering—their faces alight with what looked like genuine joy at their first glimpse of the bride.

'It'll be okay, Dad,' Lucy whispered, and squeezed his arm. 'Just pretend it's the village church.'

'I don't think my imagination is quite *that* good,' remarked her father wryly.

Lucy was wearing ivory—which flattered her Titian hair far more than pure white would have done. Anyway, she would have felt a hypocrite wearing white when both families knew she was pregnant— and soon the rest of the world would, too. There would be smug smiles all round, of that she was certain. Hadn't she scoured newspaper columns herself and done sums on her fingers to work out if a child had been conceived before or after marriage?

Her wedding gown was cut with flattering simplicity—a floor-length dress, its starkness relieved by a mere sprinkling of freshwater pearls sewn into the fabric. Over the top she wore a silk-chiffon overcoat which floated like a cloud in the breeze. Fragrant flowers were woven into her hair, and on her feet were a pair of exquisite high-heeled shoes which brought her almost up to Guido's nose.

The aisle seemed as long as a runway, yet all she could see were the groom's dark flashing eyes—a half-smile of what looked like encouragement as she made her way towards him.

'Are you okay?' he questioned softly as she joined him at the altar.

His heart was pounding. There had been a part of him which had wondered whether she would actually go through with it. Or just flounce off the island— since no one could have physically stopped her—and try to fight him through the courts for custody of the child. Had she been sensible enough to heed his words and realise that such a battle would have been lost before it had begun? Would that explain her fixed and determined smile? And was she also sensible enough to see that it was possible to make this work?

'I'm fine, thank you,' Lucy answered politely, discovering that it was easy to squash the haunting demons of bitter regret—if you practised long and hard enough.

She had decided that she was going to behave exactly as a bride should behave, and not let her parents—or herself—down. She was pregnant with Guido's child, and there were far-reaching repercussions which she had been forced to accept. She was certainly not going to start coming over like a petulant adolescent, sulking because her marriage was not the one she had sometimes dreamed of.

Oh, on the outside it was all those things—and more. Her friends had been in turn envious and disbelieving. For how many women with Lucy's background ended up marrying a devastatingly handsome prince from a picturesque Mediterranean island? How many would be made a princess the moment the ring was slid onto her finger?

Her schoolfriend, Davina, had voiced what most of the others were feeling. 'Huh—at least *you* aren't going to have to save up for ever for your reception—*or* your honeymoon!'

Lucy had allowed them all their envy—for pride had let her confide in no one that it was simply a marriage of coincidence. But it had been Lucy who had felt envious. Davina might have a few years of scrimping and saving ahead of her—of making do and pass-me-down baby equipment—but she had a fiancé who adored her, who would do anything in the world if it made her happy.

And that was the difference.

Lucy had Guido—royal and rich and powerful.

And utterly remote.

She stared into his black eyes and saw nothing there other than a look of quiet triumph and determination.

The ceremony was conducted in French as well as English—in order to satisfy Mardivinian law. And as Guido slipped the slim platinum band on her trembling finger Lucy was aware that her life was never

going to be the same again. She had left Lucy
Maguire behind at the altar and had become Princess
Lucy Jennifer Cacciatore instead.

They emerged from the cathedral to a storm of
swirling rose petals and the blinding light of flash-
bulbs, which set out in stark relief the banked flowers
lining the steps leading down to the waiting carriage.

Once the door had slammed shut on them Guido
turned to her. 'Have I told you how beautiful you
look?' he murmured.

She was feeling like a drooping flower, and not in
the least bit beautiful. 'We're alone now, Guido,' she
said tetchily. 'So you can drop the pretence.'

A pulse hammered at his temple. 'How you test
me, Lucy,' he observed steadily.

She smiled down at a small girl who had hurled a
rather battered home-grown posy into the carriage. 'I
don't see why. You've got what you wanted, haven't
you? Legally I'm your bride, but in reality I'm your
prisoner!'

'Don't be so melodramatic!' he said angrily. 'You
are free to move at liberty!'

'Oh, really? So if I took a flight back to England
tomorrow, then you'd be perfectly agreeable?'

'In theory, there would be no objection.'

'In theory?' She opened her eyes very wide, aware
that she was being prickly—but wasn't that a kind of
defence mechanism? She was trying to accept the situation for what it was, and not what she would like
it to be.

And she was trying to stop herself from loving a man who had used her right from the very start.

He gave a hard smile. 'But the doctor has advised you not to travel,' he said smoothly.

'Very conveniently for you!' she retorted. 'And I suppose that if the doctor had told me that I had to run round and round the Palace gardens every morning, no doubt you'd be behind it!'

'I think you can be assured that if I were using the doctor as my mouthpiece, then I could think of more satisfying commands to give than an early-morning run,' he murmured.

Lucy blushed, hot colour creeping all the way up her bare neck. 'That was unnecessary!'

'Really?' he questioned innocently. 'You don't know to what I was alluding.'

No, but she had a pretty good idea. Apart from Guido's one brief comment, during the run-up to the wedding they had not spoken of the physical side of their marriage. In the flurry of arrangements there had simply not been time nor the inclination—certainly not on Lucy's part. Besides, it was actually quite a difficult thing to discuss.

When you were a couple having sex you didn't discuss it—unless you were erotically describing your likes and dislikes. It was a subject which did not bear scrutiny or analysis. But they had stopped being a couple and stopped having sex a long time ago—it was only the baby which had prompted this bizarre wedding. Of *course* they were going to ignore it.

And when a subject was deliberately ignored and

not spoken about, then it became huge inside your head. Lucy found herself tortured with memories of just how good it had been…and how much had changed. It could never be the same, could it? Not now.

She turned to the squealing crowd with a wide smile which threatened to split her face in two.

'Are you intending to make this a proper marriage, Lucy?' he questioned quietly.

She moved her head back to face him. Wasn't there still some remnant of the schoolgirl idealist inside her, who did not want harsh words to mar what should have been the happiest day of her life? So that, no matter what happened in the future, she could one day say to her son—or daughter—that it *had* been a happy day.

What did he want? A submissive yes while they clip-clopped their way through the streets of Mardivino?

'Now is neither the time nor the place to discuss it, Guido!'

'As you wish, my Princess,' he mocked.

The Rainbow Palace was festooned with flowers, and a wedding breakfast was laid out in the formal Mirrored Dining Room—on which, legend had it, one of the rooms at the Palace of Versailles had been modelled. Lucy could see her bridal image reflected back from every angle. Was that pale and doe-eyed creature in a beautiful wedding dress really her?

The Crown Prince was talking to her and, with an effort, she flashed Gianferro a huge smile.

'You will eat something?' he was saying.

'I...'

Lately, her appetite had been sparrow-like, to say the least. About to refuse, she saw the look of concern on his face and nodded instead, obediently forking a sliver of some delicate, unknown fish into her mouth. She had actually lost weight. In the space of a fort-night, her wedding dress had been twice taken in by the Parisian couturier who had been flown over es-pecially to make it for her.

'It's...it's delicious,' she said.

'You are happy, Lucy?'

Gianferro's unexpected question came out of the blue. How much had Guido told him? Did he believe it to be a love-match—and, if so, did she have the right to disillusion him?

Lucy knew then that no matter what was going on inside she had made a contract with Guido for the sake of the baby. And for all their sakes she must play the part of the blushingly contented bride.

She raised her glass of fruit juice. 'I am,' she said, feeling a pang of guilt as she looked across the table at her mother, who was giggling at something Guido was saying. She smiled, so proud of her. For a woman whose calendar highlight was the church Bring-and-Buy sale, she too seemed to be adapting remarkably well. Well, she must make her mother proud of her, too. 'It's a very exciting day,' she murmured.

'Indeed it is,' he said thoughtfully. 'And Guido is taking you to the mountains for your honeymoon?'

'Yes, he is,' she agreed steadily.

'You did not long for a more traditional destination? Paris or Rome, perhaps?'

'Oh, no. I want to get to know my new country,' she said staunchly. She couldn't tell Gianferro that those cities were for ever tainted with memories of how it *had* been between them.

Then it had been sex and laughter, and a determination on her part to play the independent role required of her—but it had all backfired on her. And nothing had changed in that regard. She was still playing a role—except that now it just happened to be a different one.

'And after the honeymoon?' Gianferro's voice cut into her thoughts. 'What then?'

'We haven't decided.' Or rather, they hadn't discussed it—like so much else. She bit her lip as she glanced across the table to find Guido's black eyes on her.

He had been watching her, and saw her easy and laughing interaction with his brother change into a frozen look of *froideur* as she met his eyes. As if she was wishing herself a million miles away...

Well, you and me too, *cara*, he thought bitterly. The last thing in the world he wanted was to be incarcerated here on Mardivino, back in the whole damned strait-jacket of formality and ritual.

But it had to be.

Or did it?

Were her surroundings only adding to her feeling of entrapment? Should he reassure her on that score—tell her that their stay here need only be temporary if that was what she desired?

But he felt the cold pulse of anger as she turned her head away from him, as if he were invisible. Well, if that was the way she wanted to play it—if she intended to be stubborn—then she would soon discover that he could be stubborn, too...

Unseen beneath the damask tablecloth, Lucy's hand crept to cover the faint swell of her belly, willing herself not to succumb to the tide of emotion which was washing over her. Was it the rushing of her hormones which was making her feel so vulnerable? If so, she must be sure not to show it. Because he would not care—and why should he?

It was pointless to look for a soft response in a man like Guido. He had never behaved in that way before, so why the hell should he change now?

She watched him rise to his feet, resplendent in dark morning suit, his black hair ruffled and his olive skin gleaming. He was coming towards her, and despite everything her heart turned over. Why were emotions so impervious to logic? Why the hell did love have to leap out and grab you so inappropriately? Make you want to care for someone even though instinct told you there would be nothing coming back?

He gave a short laugh as he saw her face grow pale, and his words were so silky-soft that they could be heard by no one else.

'At least try to maintain the charade of happiness

on your wedding day, *cara*. Your mother will be distressed if you do otherwise. Come, Lucy.' He held his hand out for hers, and as she looked up at him his eyes glittered like deadly black ice. 'It is time to leave for our honeymoon.'

CHAPTER NINE

'SO TELL me, Lucy.' The black eyes glittered with challenge. 'What do a couple do on honeymoon when they aren't engaged in the rather more traditional pastime?'

From beneath her sunhat Lucy looked at him, and despite her intention not to, a shiver of pure longing ran through her. How different he looked from the man with whom she had exchanged her vows. Transformed from a formal and dark-suited elegance to a totally laid-back look, like a man happily at home on the beach.

He wore a pair of faded cut-off denims, which showed hard, muscular legs, and a thin cotton shirt which was flapping open, giving her occasional and distracting glimpses of his hair-roughened chest.

His mocking eyes were still challenging her for an answer, and she knew then that she could not keep running from the truth. She answered like the old Lucy—that self-deluding idiot who had thought she could match this man in the emotional detachment department.

The old Lucy would have met that challenge head-on. 'Are you trying to tell me you're frustrated?' she questioned.

'Well, aren't you?' he shot back.

'I have other things on my mind.'

'Such as?'

She pointed to the book which was lying open on her lap. 'You should try reading some time.'

'So should you.' His mouth twisted into an odd kind of smile. 'That's been open at the same page for the last hour!'

'I've been admiring the scenery.'

'I know you have,' he mocked.

'And what's that supposed to mean?'

He shrugged, flopping down onto the sand beside her. 'If you find the sight of my body so irresistible that you can't bear to tear your eyes away, Lucy— then stare away! Who am I to stop you?'

'I was not staring!'

'Oh, yes, you were,' he contradicted softly. 'You can't stop looking at me...just as I can't stop looking at you.'

He let his eyes drift over her, in a pale-green swim-suit which so flattered her colouring. Shaded by a hat *and* an umbrella—that fair English skin of hers would burn very easily—she was sitting rather primly on the soft, fine sand, occasionally swigging from a large bottle of cool water. The thin, stretchy material was moulded to her like a second skin, emphasising the increased swelling of her breasts and the hint of rounded belly which would grow bigger by the day.

At least she seemed less on edge today—some of the tight tension which had come so close to snapping on their wedding day seemed to have dissolved. He had seen the sadness as she bade farewell to her parents—the slight crumpling of her face which she had been so desperately trying to hide.

In that moment he had wanted to reach out and comfort her, but then he had reminded himself that he would not be able to follow through. The stone around his heart was too deeply ingrained to ever be shattered. It was better to start as he meant to go on, and he knew he could never give her real love. And maybe in that sense at least Lucy was the perfect bride for him. Wasn't that one of the things which had always fascinated him about her—the fact that she wasn't emotionally needy?

After her parents had left for England she had busied herself with changing—obviously she hadn't wanted him to see her moment of wistfulness—and when she had emerged again it had been with a pale and set face.

They had travelled to their honeymoon destination—the Cacciatore mountain lodge—and that night she had resolutely dressed in cotton pyjamas and climbed into the low divan, turning her back on him in a silent gesture which spoke volumes.

His mouth had hardened as he had gazed upwards at the moonshadows which danced on the ceiling.

Did she imagine that he was going to beg her to make love? Or that he would wait for ever for her to change her mind?

Like hell he would!

Today he had driven her to the sea, in an attempt to fill up the day with something other than the unspoken frustrations and resentments between them.

But everything seemed to be having the wrong effect. She was wearing very little, and so was he. And the trouble was that the way he felt was becoming very difficult to disguise....

Nervously, she glanced at him, seeing for herself just how aroused he was, and feeling that wretched hot, moist ache once more, tempting her to give in. She wanted him. She had never really stopped wanting him. But what good was sex going to do them now? Wouldn't it only complicate a complicated situation still further? 'Don't look at me that way,' she begged.

'What way is that? You mean, the way that any new husband would look at his wife?'

'Oh, please, Guido!' she retorted. 'We're not like a new husband and wife at all!'

'In some ways we are,' he argued softly. 'Or rather, we could be.'

She shook her head. Not the way that counted, they couldn't. 'No.'

'Then that is your decision, *cara*, not mine,' he bit out. 'And you must live with the consequences.'

She stared at him. She could see the hot light of desire which lit his dark eyes. Once that alone would have filled her with a heady kind of pride at having him within her power. But now she could see that for what it really was—a shallow and insignificant pride. Just because a man desired you physically it didn't mean anything. He could desire all kinds of people— it just depended on who happened to be there at the time. He had already proved that to her.

'You think that us having sex is going to make everything better?' she said slowly.

'In a word, yes. It would certainly make things a little more…comfortable.' He shifted slightly, and he saw her look of horrified fascination as it was drawn once more towards his shorts.

'Sex as a physical exercise, you mean? A bodily function that needs to be fulfilled—like scratching an itch?'

'Don't knock it, Lucy,' he said softly. 'You certainly never used to knock it before.'

She bit her lip and picked up the bottle to drink thirstily from it, but it did little to relieve the dryness in her mouth and she put it back down, her eyes serious. 'Aren't there other things we should be discussing, Guido? More important things?'

'Oh?' He raised his dark brows.

'Well, for a start—we haven't even decided where we're going to be living.'

He sucked in a hot, dry breath. This was part of their deal. 'You get to choose, remember?'

Never in a million years could Lucy have imagined her home as a newly-wed being decided by something as businesslike as a pre-nuptial agreement. 'I don't want to live in New York.'

'Any reason why?'

'I don't think your apartment is suitable for a baby.'

'Then we'll move somewhere that is.'

She shook her head. New York was *his* city. She had tried to imagine his life going on, and hers at home with the baby, and the idea petrified her. He wasn't going to take her out and introduce her to all his friends and play cosy-cosy, was he? Not when it would be a façade he might have difficulty maintaining.

And besides, New York was jam-packed full of temptation...

'No,' she said quietly.

'So just where *do* you want to live?'

What would he say if she suggested England? But deep down, Lucy knew that was a non-starter—and it had nothing to do with the fact that England almost seemed too small to contain him. No. Her mother would take one look at her face and would guess at her daughter's unhappiness. She couldn't do that to her.

Which left only one place—the only place where she felt safe and grounded...

'I'd like to live on Mardivino.'

Guido nodded. He should have seen this coming. He had flexed his muscles over the marriage and now she was showing that she could do the same. She knew how he felt about Royal life. Was she perhaps hoping that by incarcerating him here he would yield to her? Grant her a divorce and custody and a settlement? He gave a tight smile. She would soon learn that he could not be manipulated.

'As you wish,' he said coolly.

Lucy frowned. She had expected more reaction than that. Her explanation had been rehearsed; she was just waiting for his terse interrogation. But it seemed he had no interest in hearing it. Just what did she have to do to get a reaction from him?

Talk about the things that counted, that was what. 'You know,' she said softly, 'there's something which we've avoided talking about altogether.'

'I can hardly wait,' he drawled sardonically. 'Do enlighten me.'

Was he being deliberately unperceptive? Or was he just in denial? 'The baby, of course!' The tiny creature which was growing in her belly even now. Growing, but almost unacknowledged—certainly up until now. But maybe they were all in denial.

Even her mother had only fleetingly referred to it. Was it delicacy which had prevented her—an old-fashioned idea that a shotgun marriage should not be seen as that? As if the honeymoon was going to wipe the slate clean so they could come back, the bad start would be forgotten and only then could they begin to discuss the forthcoming child?

'*Our* baby,' she added softly.

He stared hard and unseeingly at the sea. 'There is nothing to discuss.'

'Of course there is!' But she was unprepared for the look on his face when he turned it back to her. She had always thought of Guido as cold and remote, but now it was as if someone had chiselled his features from some dark, icy rock. She drew back from the look, startled. 'What is it?' she whispered.

He banished the nebulous fears which swirled like dark clouds around his mind and recovered himself. 'I thought that everything had been decided. You will be cared for by the finest obstetricians, and the baby will be born here on Mardivino.'

How cold-blooded he sounded! But he *is* cold-blooded, she reminded herself. 'And then?'

'Who knows what then? There are a million things which could happen between now and then. The most important thing,' he added savagely, 'is to ensure the baby's safety. And your own,' he finished, on a harsh note.

A forgotten memory flew into her mind. Was he thinking about his own mother and her confinement with Nico? For hadn't it been his birth which had heralded her death, resulting in the fracturing of the family? A Royal family, yes—with all the back-up and support that their wealth and position could provide—but no less vulnerable than any other young family.

She wanted to reach her hand out to touch him— not in a sexual way, more a comforting and reassuring one—to tell him that there was no reason that history should repeat itself. But his frozen and forbidden stance stopped her.

And, God forgive her, something terrible had occurred to her. If she died then she might briefly be grieved for by him as the baby's mother, but nothing else. She would be out of the way. No obstacle to his wishes or desires any more.

He felt rather than saw her shiver, and slowly turned his head to find a look of indescribable pain lurking in the back of her eyes. And this he found he could not ignore.

'What is wrong?' he questioned softly.

'How long have you got?' She shook her head, recognising that he had hit the nail on the head earlier—her thoughts really *could* be described as melodramatic. She forced them back to the real problems they faced and looked at him. 'How about the fact that we're both sitting on a beautiful beach and wishing we could be anywhere else on earth but here?'

'Is that what you wish?'

No. She wished for the impossible. That his face would soften with love and not just longing. That their baby had been conceived amid the flow of some emotion other than a wild and unstoppable desire. But that was like a child wishing for make-believe.

'I'm trying to imagine the future,' she said desperately. 'And I just can't.'

'But no one ever can, Lucy,' he said quietly. 'And you shouldn't even try. It rarely turns out as you imagine it to. It's the present you have to hang on to.'

Maybe that was even more difficult. This was the present, and she was all over the place, not knowing how to react or what to say. Unsure whether it would be right or wrong to succumb to him physically—whether that would improve their relationship or simply make her more aware of its glaring deficiencies.

'We don't even know one another!' she said desperately. 'Not really.'

He was silent for a moment. 'If you presented that problem to a third party, then they would say that the obvious solution is to try.'

'How?'

'You could start by not turning your back on me in bed. By not flinching when I come close to you.'

They were talking, she realised, at cross purposes. She was talking about peeling away all the layers that people protected themselves with—especially in his case—to find the real person who lay beneath.

Guido, on the other hand, was talking about something entirely different. 'It isn't just about sex!'

'But isn't sex a good place to start? To hold one another, to feel close to one another?'

It wasn't real closeness, but would it do? Wasn't it better to have something which masqueraded as intimacy rather than no intimacy at all?

Lucy nodded as she came to a decision, swallowing down the lump of apprehension which had stuck like an acrid rock in the back of her throat. She struggled to find the words which would allow her to keep her dignity—maybe even make him think that the Lucy who had enjoyed sex without involvement hadn't been real either. 'Very well,' she said quietly. 'I'll consent to having sex with you.'

A look of indescribable fury crossed over his face, making him look like the devil incarnate. 'You'll *consent*?' he questioned incredulously. 'You will *consent* to having sex with me?'

'I didn't mean it the way it came out!'

'Oh, on the contrary, Lucy,' he said icily. 'I think that's exactly what you meant.' He scrambled to his feet, the sun behind him making him into a forbidding silhouette which dominated her horizon. She couldn't see his face now, but she didn't need to—the bitter quality of his voice spoke volumes.

'Well, you must forgive me if I decline your delightful *offer*. I have never had a woman who has to endure sex with me, and I have no intention of starting now.'

'Guido, listen—'

'No, you *listen*!' He cut through her words, and for the first time she saw him as truly and ominously imperious. A distant and powerful prince with everyone in the world eager to do his bidding. 'I told you when you agreed to marry me—'

'Agreed?' She gave a bitter laugh. 'You mean when you forced my hand?'

'I told you,' he continued furiously, 'that the terms of the marriage itself would be up to you. So if you're planning to act like a Victorian wife and lie back and think of England—you can forget it! Either I have a warm and giving woman in my bed, or none at all!'

'And if none at all?' she questioned steadily. 'Are you planning to seek your comfort elsewhere?'

He bent down then, and now she *could* see his face. She could almost feel the fierce heat from the hot and angry fire in his eyes.

'What do you think, Lucy?' he hissed. 'That I'll settle for a life of celibacy?'

She stared at him unhappily. They had reached, she realised, a stalemate.

CHAPTER TEN

THEY cut the honeymoon short, of course. They had to—for the sake of their sanity.

After their bitter row on the beach, a state of silent and frozen warfare descended, which made their enforced proximity almost unbearable.

Guido went out of his way to avoid her whenever he could. He spent an inordinate amount of time sailing and running and swimming—coming back each day worn out by the sheer physical endurance with which he had tested himself to his limits.

And he had a dark look of simmering rage whenever he looked at her.

Lucy, meanwhile, carried on pretending to read her book—even going to the trouble of turning several handfuls of pages by the time he returned.

But he was not easily fooled.

'Want to tell me what the story's all about?' he challenged mockingly one evening, and her face flushed scarlet as she snapped it closed.

'We can't go on like this,' she said on their fourth evening, when he had just arrived back from a lone trip to the beach and she had been pacing around like a caged lion.

He was right—when a couple weren't doing what

they were traditionally supposed to do on honeymoon it left an awful lot of awkward hours to fill.

He was raking his fingers through the black tendrils of his hair, all sea-damp and knotted from his swim. On the broad bank of his shoulders was the faintest sprinkling of fine white sand, which contrasted alluringly against the deep olive skin. A pair of shorts which were moulded like rubber to the hard curve of his buttocks were the only brief barrier against his nakedness.

He turned his head to look at her, enjoying the discomfiture on her face. Deliberately he jutted his hips forward and saw her colour deepen.

'I agree,' he said smoothly. 'We can't. Shall we pack up and go back to Solajoya?'

Lucy blinked. Just like that? Had she hoped for another discussion—perhaps one with a different outcome this time? One which might see them ending up in bed and letting passion wash away much of the discord?

There's nothing to stop you going over to him now, mocked a voice in her head.

But there was—of course there was. The distance between them had grown so wide, she could imagine nothing which would bring them back together again. Instead, she was forced to endure the terrible hunger that gnawed away inside her.

And why did he not approach *her*? She had swallowed her pride once and offered to break the deadlock. Hadn't it been his arrogant dismissal of her fumbling offer which had caused all this bitterness to surface?

She shrugged. 'If you want.'

He gave a short laugh. As if she cared what he wanted!

'Guido?'

He met her eyes. 'What is it, my Princess?'

'Do you think that we can start being…?'

Being what? he wondered. Lovers? He raised his eyebrows imperiously. 'Well, what is it, Lucy?' he questioned softly. 'What do you want us to be?'

Friends seemed too much to ask for in the current circumstances, but surely there was a springboard from which things could move on—however slowly—and get better between them. 'Civil,' she said. 'To each other.'

Civil. He thought that she had a curious choice of words at times. It was an oddly mechanical description. Or maybe not. She was, after all, describing the workings of a marriage. Did she not realise how much she was asking of him?

'I think I can just about manage civility,' he murmured.

She nodded, breathless in that moment as peace briefly swam in the air around them.

'Do you want to wait outside?' he questioned softly, and looped his thumbs inside the waistband of his shorts. 'Because I'm just about to remove these.'

His calculated remark shattered that elusive calm, and Lucy left as swiftly as someone who had never seen a naked man before, banging the door behind her and hearing his mocking laughter ringing in her ears.

She drew in several deep and faltering breaths of the pure air as she stared at the picturesque mountains which dominated the skyline. The startling peaks were turning deepest blue and indigo against the flame of the setting sun, yet Lucy was immune to their beauty. She felt like someone in a spacecraft, viewing the earth from a long, long way away. Totally disconnected.

She placed a palm over her swelling belly and closed her eyes. Only her baby seemed real in this make-believe world she inhabited.

That morning there had been the merest butterfly fluttering—too fleeting and insubstantial to know whether it was movement or just indigestion. And she had felt an unbearable wave of sadness. If only things had been different she would have called him over, and he would have pressed his hand there and they would have held their breath, eyes meeting, smiling the complicit smiles of parents-to-be.

As it was, she had said nothing—just made a pot of herbal tea to distract herself.

Oddly enough, when they drove into Solajoya the Rainbow Palace seemed welcoming—who would ever have thought she would be so glad to see the grand and glittering building? Yet it felt like home.

Or maybe that was because Nico and Ella came running out to meet them.

'You're back early!' Ella exclaimed.

'Morning sickness,' said Lucy, not daring to meet Guido's eyes.

'But you're feeling much better now that you're back, aren't you, Lucy?' questioned Guido smoothly.

'But how was it?' asked Ella excitedly, linking her arm through Lucy's in a sisterly way. The physical contact was oddly moving and made Lucy want to start to cry. 'Aren't the mountains the most beautiful you've ever seen?'

Instinct made her nod, but then Nico made things a million times worse.

'Oh, Ella,' he purred, with a grin. 'I don't imagine that they will have done much sightseeing!'

And Lucy *did* look up then, straight into the mocking dark ice of Guido's eyes.

Gianferro's stern face softened when he saw Lucy.

'You are keeping well?' he questioned.

Lucy nodded. 'Oh, yes,' she said staunchly, as if her very life depended on it. 'Very well.'

And, of course, there was Leo—gorgeous, gurgling Leo—who Lucy couldn't resist.

Guido came to the Nursery bathroom one day, just as Lucy was towelling him dry. She had suds in her hair and her face was rosy, and she looked up from blowing raspberries on Leo's plump little stomach to find her husband standing in the doorway watching her, some indefinable emotion flitting across his face. But she reminded herself that Guido didn't do emotion.

'Nico and Ella have gone out for lunch,' she said, by way of an explanation he had not asked for.

He frowned. 'And there is no nursemaid?'

She pinned a nappy in place—there were no new-fangled disposables at the Palace—and looked up at him. 'It's her day off, and besides—I like doing it.'

The way she was kneeling made the size of her growing bump quite unmistakable, and he wondered how she managed to look so sexy when she was dripping with water and dealing with a squirming baby. He felt the jack-knifing of desire. God, if he had to endure a second longer of this hot-house of frustration then he would burst.

'You have to have something to fill your day, I guess.'

She nodded. It wasn't a very subtle barb, but she would ignore it. She certainly wasn't going to have a row when there was a little baby around. All the child care books—which she was currently devouring—said that babies were very susceptible to the atmosphere around them. Which did not bode very well for the future.

'I need as much practice as I can get, of course.'

'Of course,' he echoed. He stood there for a moment or two longer and then said, 'I have to fly to New York.'

Her fingers stilled in the act of buttoning the crisp lawn romper suit, and she looked up, feeling the blood drain from her face. 'To New York?' she questioned dully.

'That's right.'

'Oh?' Her voice trembled. 'Any reason why?'

He smiled. 'I have business to attend to—why else?'

A couple of reasons sprang to mind, and one of them was disturbing enough to make her tremble. But if she challenged him he would only deny them, and then it would look as if she didn't trust him.

But she *didn't* trust him!

He paused, still standing like a dark, carved statue by the door. 'You could always come with me.'

The suggestion was made from the other side of the bathroom—not a million miles away, though it might as well have been.

Lucy tried to imagine what it would be like—just the two of them on his territory, with Guido busying himself with work while she was trapped in that vast luxury apartment. At least here in Mardivino she felt comfortable—surrounded by family who seemed to like her.

She shook her head. 'I don't know if it would be a good idea to travel in my—'

'Condition?' he mocked softly. 'Oh, come, come, Lucy—you can't use the baby as an excuse for everything! I thought that the modern way was for women to climb mountains in the latter stages!'

'I'm happy here,' she said stubbornly.

'Yes.' He flicked her a thoughtful look. 'You seem to have taken to being a princess with a passion.'

Lucy sat back on her heels. 'What's that supposed to mean?'

He smiled, but it was a hard, cruel smile. 'Just that I guess the luxuries of Royal life must go some way towards compensating for other areas which are somewhat…lacking.'

Was he accusing her? Of taking to her role rather too well? When all the while she had wanted him to be proud of her…

She picked Leo up. 'And how long will you be away?'

The dark eyebrows were elevated. 'Why?'

'*Why?* Because you're my husband and I have a right to know!'

His mouth tightened. 'I wouldn't get into a conversation about "rights", if I were you,' he said acidly. 'And I don't know why you refer to me as your husband.' The black eyes burnt into her. 'We may be married, but in all the ways that matter I am certainly not your husband.'

CHAPTER ELEVEN

GUIDO had gone, and Lucy's world suddenly felt as though there was a large and vital chunk of it missing. But things became much clearer without his disturbing presence.

Lucy realised that she had placed far too much importance on distracting herself from what was happening within their marriage, and that in a way it had been all too easy. There was always something going on—other family to talk to, and servants who had a habit of appearing, putting paid to tense atmospheres. And there were lunches and dinners and receptions which filled enough of her life to keep her relatively contented.

Or so she had thought.

Yet without Guido around all these things became meaningless. Nico and Ella had their real life together, with their son, and Gianferro was busy ruling the Principality. Lucy was just an observer—a shadowy figure on the outside—trying to join in but having no real part to play. And she wanted her husband to come back.

She began to obsess about his real reasons for going. He had cited work, but he could work from anywhere—he had only to pick up the phone.

There had been no physical contact at all between

them—and no sign that the deadlock would ever be broken. So had he decided that enough was enough? That while she might accept this loveless marriage he certainly would not?

She stared out at the Palace gardens, where autumn was beginning to rob the landscape of the last of the flowers, and she bit back the sob which was forming in her throat. She might as well have given her written permission for him to go away and have an affair with someone!

Whose advice could she ask? No one's. That was the trouble. No one to tell, or to confide in. Oh, she liked Ella a lot, and they got along just fine. But Ella was her sister-in-law and she would be bound to tell Nico, and then everyone would know how bad things were between her and Guido.

And wouldn't that destabilise everyone—especially with the King lying there, so sick?

She turned away from the gardens to look at herself in the mirror. Her bump was really very noticeable now, though the rest of her was still very slim. In fact, it was only from the side that you could really tell she was pregnant at all. She was wearing jeans and a beautiful floaty shirt made of velvet and silk and bits of feather, which she had bought in one of Solajoya's more exclusive boutiques.

Her skin was the clearest it had ever been and her eyes were as shining as her hair. In some ways she had never looked better. Pregnancy suited her, as did the clean air of Mardivino and the wonderful fresh food which was served to her every day.

But all this meant nothing. She had allowed the distance between herself and Guido to flourish and grow, with each trying to outdo the other in terms of stubbornness. If a stalemate had been reached, then someone had to break it. And if Guido was too proud then it would have to be her. And wasn't it only fear which was stopping her? The fear that if she let him get close to her then it would open up the floodgates around her heart and let out all those feelings she had bottled up?

She bit her lip. He had been gone over a week now. Maybe it was too late. Maybe even now he was in bed with another sooty-eyed blonde—someone who didn't 'mean' anything, but who could provide him with the physical comfort his wife was steadfastly refusing to give.

Pain and regret and jealousy lanced through her heart and she closed her eyes before coming to a decision.

She would fly to New York!

Obviously she'd need to clear it with Gianferro first, but what was the point of being a princess if you couldn't just fly to America on a whim? But she would beg Gianferro's silence, for she wanted it to be a surprise.

She just prayed it would be a pleasant one…

The sound of the doorbell punctured the sultry wail of the music, and Guido narrowed his eyes with irritation. Who the hell was that, and why the hell had they been allowed up? He had specifically told the porter that he did not want to be disturbed....

It pealed again. Unbelievable! He rose to his feet and pulled open the door, unable to make the connection for a moment. It was a bit like seeing an iceberg in the middle of the desert—completely unexpected. The very last thing he had expected was to see his wife standing on the doorstep.

'Hello, Guido,' she said quietly.

'Lucy!' He raised his eyebrows. 'This is certainly a surprise.'

It wasn't the greeting she had wanted or hoped for. He was standing there with a wary look on his face, yet his hard, lean body was tense and expectant.

'Maybe I should have phoned. Aren't you going to invite me in?' And then she stopped focussing on him and focussed on the sound of sultry saxophone drifting through the air from behind him. Her eyes opened wide in horror. 'Unless...unless—' Oh, God. 'Unless you're busy, of course?'

He heard the accusation in her voice and his mouth tightened. 'And what is it you think I might be busy with, Lucy?' he questioned, in a soft, dangerous voice. 'You think I have someone in here with me?'

The world stood still. She looked into his eyes, black and stormy as the night. 'Have you?'

'Why don't you take a look for yourself?'

She needed courage then as she had never needed it before, and she brushed past him, her head held high, two wings of colour burning across her cheeks.

The room looked set for seduction. Soft lights. Soft

music. There was even a bottle of wine opened. Her eyes scanned the table. One glass! She turned back to look at him again, only this time his eyes were taunting her.

'Seen enough?' he mocked.

She had come to a tentative decision on the plane, and the emotions which were rollercoastering around inside her now made it crystallise into certainty. She was through with treading carefully, as if she was negotiating some rocky and unknown path. From now on she was going to start walking proud and strong.

'Are you alone?' she demanded.

He gave an odd kind of laugh and walked over to the table. He poured himself a glass of wine, glancing over his shoulder at her. 'Will you join me?' he questioned, in a mocking voice.

He still hadn't answered her question! But surely his careless attitude must mean that there was no one else in the apartment? Not even Guido could demonstrate *sang-froid* like that if some female was hiding out in the bedroom. The thought of that made her wince.

'I'm pregnant!' she said, relief making her snap at him. 'Remember?'

'How am I likely to forget?' he lobbed back, and then sipped his wine. 'Sit down. Take the weight off your feet and tell me why you're here.'

Lucy sank onto one of the sofas, suddenly exhausted. Why *was* she here?

'Or let me guess,' he continued. 'You thought you would turn up unannounced to ''surprise'' me, but in reality you were expecting to catch me in bed with someone—isn't that right, Lucy?'

The strain had been building up for a long time, and now it had reached an unbearable pitch. His words were enough to make her snap. She stared at him, all pretence gone, for she did not have the appetite or the energy for it any more. 'Yes!' she cried. 'Yes, I did! Yes, yes, yes—I did!'

His face was a cruel, dark mask. 'And that would have played right into your hands, wouldn't it? For, no matter how watertight a prenuptial agreement, what court is going to look kindly on a man who is unfaithful to his young pregnant bride within the first month of marriage? Was that why you refused to have sex with me, Lucy? Hoping to drive me to just that response? Because, if so, I hate to disappoint you— but on this occasion I'm going to have to. Feel free to search every nook and cranny of the apartment, but you will find it empty.'

She had thought that she could not be hurt any more than she already had been, but she had been wrong, for his wounding words slashed right through what remained of her composure. Did he really think she was so scheming that she would concoct such a thing? That she would use their sex-life—or lack of it—as some strategy—a carefully devised plan? Did he think so little of her that he thought she was capable of such deviousness?

A long, shuddering cry escaped her, and, willing the tears not to fall, she buried her face in her hands.

'Lucy?'

She heard the concern in his voice but shook her head as if to deny it, her hair spilling untidily over her shoulders.

'*Lucy!*' he said urgently, and then he was by her side.

'Go away.'

'Look at me.'

'No!' Her words were muffled by her hands, and as she felt him draw them away she stared at him defiantly. 'I didn't scheme, if that's what you think, but, yes, I did think you might have someone here—or that you might in the future. And what's more…what is more…who could really blame you if you did?'

He stilled. '*What did you just say?* That sounded very like you giving me permission to stray, *cara*.' His voice took on a deadly tone. 'Is that what you would like? To free me so that another man can be your lover? Do you have someone in mind, then, Lucy?'

How wrong could he possibly be? 'No!' She stared at him as if he were completely mad. 'I haven't wanted anyone else! Not since I met you—not for a second.'

'Then perhaps you would explain what it is you're talking about?'

She shrugged her shoulders desperately. 'I know that you're a hot-blooded man—and I had no right to withhold sex from you.'

'Oh, for God's sake—there you go again!' he exploded. 'I don't want it to *be* like that. It isn't something that *I* want and *you* won't give me—it should be something we both want. And you don't, do you, Lucy?'

There was a long, long silence. Was she strong enough to do something to rectify a situation which was becoming daily more unbearable? Or was stupid, stubborn pride going to stand in her way?

'Yes, I do,' she whispered. 'I want you very much.'

Her words were soft and indistinct, but he heard them, and he smoothed back the mussed hair from her cheeks to see confusion in her eyes.

'Oh, Lucy,' he said softly.

'I don't know how it's come to this,' she admitted on a whisper.

And neither did he. He rippled his fingers down her neck and her eyelids fluttered to a close. 'You are worn out,' he said unsteadily.

'Yes.'

'Come. Come with me.'

Her eyes flew open as he bent to scoop her up into his arms—as if he carried pregnant women every day of the week. 'Are you taking me to…bed?'

His eyes were smoky with hunger and his blood was on fire with need. Expectation was racing over his skin and making it burn. 'Oh, I think I have to— don't you?'

She was trembling and excited and scared all at the same time as he carried her through to the vast and airy room, where he lay her down on the bed. His eyes narrowed as he took in her chalk-white complexion, the freckles standing out in bold relief on her skin, as if they had been painted on. Unexpectedly he began stroking her cheek, using rhythmical, soothing fingers, as if he were petting a pampered cat, and gradually the tension began to leave her. The hectic glitter left her eyes and she felt herself sinking into the comfort zone which her keyed-up body craved, her weighted eyelids sinking irrevocably downwards.

To her astonishment, she must have slept, for when she opened her eyes again the room was empty.

Had she dreamt it all? Blinking, she sat up and looked at the empty space on the bed beside her. It was smooth and unrumpled. There was a glass of water on the bedside table and she gulped it down thirstily. When she glanced up again it was to see his dark, silent form in the doorway, watching her from between narrowed eyes.

Carefully, she put the empty glass back down. 'How long have I been asleep?'

'Two hours.'

'Two *hours*?' She stared at him. So he had changed his mind—when the opportunity had presented itself he had not wanted to make love to her after all.

He saw the look on her face and began to unbutton his shirt.

Her hand flew to suddenly trembling lips. 'Guido?'

'Mmm?' His voice was husky and deep with desire. 'You want this, Lucy,' he murmured. 'In fact, I'd say that you need it. We both do.'

There was no affection in those words, but right then she didn't care. Her mouth bone-dry, she watched as the shirt fluttered to the floor and he began to tug at his belt. He rasped the zip down and stepped out of his trousers, kicking his shoes off until he was standing proudly and unselfconsciously naked before her.

Lucy began to tremble even more—and she was not a trembling kind of person. She had seen him aroused many times, but never like this. He was walking towards her now, his face full of purpose and desire, and some soft inner core of her wanted to cry out, to ask where the tenderness of earlier had disappeared to. But he was right. Her need was as deep as his. And no words came other than the breathy sound of his name on her lips.

'Guido.'

With a fierce look of concentration, he began to undress her with hands which were steady—until she too was naked, and then they began to shake as he saw the evidence of how lush she was with his child. Her once-flat belly was now a proud, hard swell, and he felt his throat tighten as he looked at it. Should they be doing this? After her long flight and such a stormy reunion? Was it…was it *safe*? Instinct fought with desire, but desire conquered him as she lifted her arms up to loop themselves around his neck and pull him down close to her.

He gasped, as her warm, expanded body pressed against his flesh. It was a new and profoundly shattering sensation, and blindly he reached for one of the cashmere blankets which lay at the end of the bed and pushed its soft folds against her skin.

'Cover yourself!' he commanded unsteadily.

She could feel him moving away from her, but she gripped his arm tight, forcing their eyes to meet.

'You don't want me?'

'Are you crazy? Of course I want you! But I didn't realise...' He swallowed. '*Signora Dolce*, but it is a long time since I saw you naked, Lucy.'

'Too long.' One barrier had fallen down to be replaced by another, but she was damned if she was going to allow him to put her on the untouchable pedestal of the Madonna. 'And too long since we have been together like this.'

'You want me?' he demanded unsteadily. 'You are sure?'

More than anything. But she was too choked with emotion to speak for a moment. She had never seen her Guido look so undecided. 'Yes,' she breathed eventually. 'Oh, yes, I'm sure. Very sure.' And she watched his doubts dissolve.

Like an explorer discovering uncharted land, he ran the flat of his hand over her hard, pregnant swell. After a while she put her hand between his legs, and he groaned.

It felt strange and wonderful. Both disconnected and real to rediscover his flesh and his firm, hard body, to let him work the magic he always worked, as she did on him. In bed they were still dynamite together, even when she was clumsier than usual with the baby. They locked their legs around each other with the delight of familiarity sharpened by the hunger of abstinence, and their kisses were breathless.

He pulled his head away and looked down into her

face, his expression sombre. 'I am afraid of hurting you, *cara*.'

She shook her head. 'Well, you won't.' In bed, he never hurt her.

'Will you show me?' he whispered.

She could hear the uncertainty in his voice and she reached down to guide him inside her, thinking that he had sounded almost *vulnerable*. Oh, please stay like that, my darling, she prayed silently. Please.

And afterwards they lay, sucking in greedy breaths of air, Lucy in that state of sleepy satisfaction she had almost forgotten. She turned to look at him, and yawned. 'Bet you've never made love to a pregnant woman before!'

He frowned as he ran his fingertips over her bump again, only this time it was like a doctor checking for broken bones. 'Do you feel okay?'

'Guido, I feel *fine*.' And then her heart sank in disbelief as he pulled away from her and got up off the bed. 'Where do you think you're going?'

He pulled on a towelling wrap and gave her a careless smile.

'To make you some food.'

'Guido, I don't want anything to eat!' I want *you*. I want us to make things right between us—and nothing else matters apart from that.

He was running—from what, he didn't know. And what was more, he didn't care. 'You ate...when?'

She sighed. 'There was food on the plane—'

'Which you never eat—you told me yourself you

hate airline food!' he declared softly. 'Now, no protests, please, Lucy—you must look after yourself.'

Pointless to argue, for she recognised the determination in his voice. Some women might just have lain back against the down pillows and rejoiced in being waited on, but all Lucy could feel was a great, aching gap. With that one distancing gesture he had reminded her that she wouldn't even be here if it weren't for the baby. Yet they had just come together in an act that had been as much about reconciliation as making love, and that was a start. Surely the food could have waited while they talked about it?

But Guido didn't want to talk about it—and certainly not straight after sex, when his defences were down.

In the distance, she could hear him clattering around in the kitchen, even singing to himself softly in Italian, like a man well pleased with himself. But of course he would be. One fundamental appetite had been satisfied; he was now simply addressing another one.

Or was she being a little hard on him? Perhaps he needed to collect his thoughts after what had happened.

He returned to the bedroom carrying a tray loaded with coffee and sandwiches.

'You're doing my old job!' she joked. 'You'll be wearing a stewardess's uniform next!'

He smiled, but it was nothing more than a distant and sexy smile.

'Eat something,' he murmured. 'You'll feel better.'

Better?

He put the tray down to plant a long and lingering kiss on her lips, and it had the desired effect of making her skin shiver with longing. But his next words killed it stone-dead.

'Just because we have a marriage which was born out of practicality,' he said softly, 'doesn't mean to say we can't make it work—does it, Lucy?'

Her blood ran cold, for it was such an analytical and businesslike assessment, and at that precise moment Lucy realised nothing had changed. He could have been a million miles away from her instead of in the same bedroom. They might have become close in the physical sense, but that was all.

Emotionally, the stalemate remained exactly the same—with her wanting more than her cool Prince of a husband was prepared to give.

CHAPTER TWELVE

THEY stayed put in New York.

'Don't you want to be away from my family for a while?' Guido whispered beguilingly. 'Just the two of us?'

'Y-yes,' she said uncertainly—but how could she even think straight with him dipping his head to run his lips with a butterfly brush down her neck like that?

'We can fix you up with an obstetrician here, if that's what you're worried about.'

Well, actually, it wasn't—but in a way it was easier to hide behind the natural anxieties of a mother-to-be than the concerns which still lay like a steel barrier between them.

What had happened to walking proud and strong? She had come up against a rock, that was what. The stony and unchangeable knowledge that you couldn't control someone. You couldn't *make* someone love you.

Lucy nodded her head, as if her doctor's appointment had been what was troubling her all along.

He introduced her to his life in the city. His friends. His business colleagues. They went to England for Christmas to visit her parents in their rambling cottage, where they had spent a Christmas which had not proved to be the endurance test she had been dread-

ing. But then Guido had been charming and diplo-
matic—skills which had been drummed into him from
the cradle—and her mother and father had not even
begun to guess at the great emotional distance which
lay between them like a canyon.

Back in New York, there were trips to the opera
and weekends out of town. And he took her shopping—he liked taking her shopping—even though she
tried to curb the amount of clothes and jewels he lav-
ished on her.

'Guido, I don't *need* all this stuff!' she protested.

'Well, no one ever said you *needed* diamonds,' he
remarked drily. 'But I thought they were what every
woman wanted.'

Were they? Her fingers touched the icy splendour
of the huge diamond pendant which dangled between
her swollen breasts. A glittering trophy whose cost
she didn't even dare to think about. Would it sound
ungrateful to say that sometimes she felt like a little
girl who was being given free access to the dressing-
up box?

The maternity clothes she wore were cut to cleverly
flatter the bump and were shockingly expensive. But
as a princess she knew that she needed to look the
part. She couldn't attend all the functions Guido took
her to making do with a couple of well-worn and
practical maternity outfits, as most of her school-
friends seemed to have to.

She could have coped with Guido's extravagance—
with almost anything—if only his behaviour towards
her had evolved into something deeper, closer—but

it hadn't. Oh, on one level, things were vastly improved—they did the things that most married couples did now, and regular sex seemed to have made some of his tension disappear. And hers too, if she was being honest. She had made a vow that first night that she was no longer going to use sex as a bartering tool. Apart from anything else, it was counterproductive in Guido's case.

Resolutely, she put aside her doubts and her fears, and the nagging insecurity that one day he might fall truly in love with another woman and then—contract of marriage or not—it would all be over.

It didn't matter how tenderly she held him during the night—the true closeness she yearned for somehow evaded them. She felt as though she was playing a part again—only this time the part of young, pregnant bride.

When they were out together she could see people looking at them, sighing wistfully—and part of her could see why. They made a textbook couple, and she was the textbook working woman who had ended up with a fairytale marriage. If only they knew that her husband had never once told her he loved her and that she did not dare to tell him how much—despite all the odds—she loved him.

For love was blind to reason. It wasn't a balance sheet on which you weighed up all the pros and cons of why you should or should not love someone. Either you did or you didn't, and Lucy did.

Sometimes she wanted to burrow deep into that cold, clever mind of his and ask him what he really *felt* about her—except that such a question would sound like the mark of a desperate woman. And what if he told her the truth? Could she face the rest of her life living with it?

She stared at him one morning when they were finishing breakfast. Guido was scanning the financial pages of the newspapers, though she sometimes wondered why he bothered. He had all the wealth a man could want and more—and yet it was never enough. He always seemed to have the burning need to prove himself. To keep climbing the slippery slope of success, even though he had already conquered it.

'Guido?'

'Mmm?' His eyes were watchful as he glanced up from his newspaper, but this morning she seemed composed enough. He was never quite sure what kind of a mood she was going to be in—but he put that down to her hormones. In a way, he would be glad when the pregnancy was over and they could address the matter of just how their life was going to be lived from then on.

'I want to go back to Mardivino.'

A small frown pleated his forehead. 'What is your hurry, *cara*?'

'I thought the baby had to be born there.'

'So it does…but—'

'Well, I'm not allowed to fly after thirty-six weeks, and can only fly then if I have a doctor's note,' she said crisply.

He felt the violent pounding of his heart as he stared into her eyes, realising with a start that the time was almost upon them. Had he been deliberately putting it out of his mind? And did all prospective fathers—even normal ones—feel this powerful and rather terrifying realisation that their lives were never going to be the same again?

'Well, that's no problem. If we can't take a scheduled flight I'll charter a plane, or we'll get Nico to fly out from Mardivino closer to the time. He is a fine pilot.'

The last thing she wanted to talk about was his brother's dexterity with a joystick! It was Guido's reluctance to fly home which disturbed her more than anything. Was he hoping to win her round so that she would adapt to motherhood in his adopted city?

'We can't, Guido,' she said practically. 'Airlines, even private jets, impose rules like this for a very good reason. They don't want to risk a woman giving birth early—which they can. Imagine if the baby was born thirty-five thousand feet up?'

His eyes narrowed. Over his dead body! 'Very well,' he said coolly. 'We will return to the Principality.'

It was the wrong time to ask it, but Lucy was fed up with always waiting for a right time which never seemed to come. 'And…afterwards? What are we going to do then?'

There was an uneasy silence. 'How would you feel about bringing the baby up here, Lucy?'

'In New York?'

'Why not? They do have babies here, you know.'

So her suspicions had been right all along. Well,

she couldn't. She just couldn't. New York was a wonderful place, but here she felt like an outsider in a way she never had done on Mardivino.

She shook her head. 'This apartment isn't right for a young child.'

'Then we'll move further out! Buy a big house with a garden. Think about it, Lucy.'

She didn't need to; she already had. She wanted a safe harbour for her and for the baby. A flare of stubbornness reared its head, for this was, after all, *her* part of the pre-nuptial. That *she* got to choose where they would live.

'No, Guido,' she said doggedly. 'I want to go back to Mardivino.'

He slammed the newspaper down on the table. She had made it unshakably clear where she stood. He turned away and gave a wry, slightly bitter smile. She certainly wasn't letting him think that she was one of those women who followed her man to the ends of the earth. But then, only women in love did that, and she had never given him any indication of being that. Not even before all this happened...

She had never been like other women, with their wistful sighs and hints about the future. That had been one of the things he had admired about her—her no-nonsense independence.

And now?

He shook his head, trying to rid it of the mists of damnable confusion.

'Very well,' he said curtly. 'We'll fly back to the

island at the end of the week. And who knows? You might feel differently once you've had the baby.'

She opened her mouth to say that she wouldn't, but then shut it again, rubbing her fingertips distractedly at her temples.

Spring had come early to Mardivino, and Lucy's breath caught in her throat as the plane descended towards Solajoya, for there were fields of yellow, purple and white flowers. It was like a miniature world all on its own, she thought—a place where you could see beaches and mountains at the same time.

Yet now, as she looked down at the island, which was growing larger as the plane descended, she realised that Mardivino had crept in and captured some of her heart. It was as much her home as anywhere now, for her child was to be born here. A sudden wave of emotion rocked her, as if she was one of those tiny, vulnerable little boats which were bobbing around in the harbour beneath.

'Oh, Guido,' she sighed. 'Just look at it.'

But he was not looking at the view, which he had seen countless times before. His associations with flying home had never been happy ones. He preferred to look at Lucy. At the way her lips had parted, and the way she seemed suddenly to have come to life, trembling with an excited kind of anticipation.

She really *had* taken to life as Princess, he thought wryly, but especially here. In New York it didn't mean much—it was only another title—but on Mardivino itself she had real power and real status.

Things which obviously meant more to her than the husband she had been forced to marry...

As soon as they arrived at the Rainbow Palace Guido turned to her. 'I'm going to see my father,' he said briefly. 'I'll see you at dinner.'

Lucy watched him go, feeling their closeness—however superficial it had been—evaporating into the warm spring air.

At least the others seemed overjoyed to see her. Ella was chattering with excitement, and Lucy saw Gianferro's hard face relax with relief when he saw her.

'Why, you are blooming, Lucy,' he observed with a smile. 'The pregnancy progresses well, I understand?'

'Very well.'

'And how was New York?'

'Oh, it was just like New York,' she said lightly. 'It's good to be...back.'

'Indeed,' he agreed, and although a look of curiosity flashed into his black eyes he said nothing.

Lucy was walking around the Palace gardens on a warm, bright afternoon when the first pains began, and she doubled over, trying like crazy to shallow breathe, as she'd been taught.

Stopping every few minutes, she managed to make her way back to their suite and Guido was brought to her. Concern and fear etched deep shadows on his hard face as he saw the doctor bending over her.

'Come e?' he demanded.

'Highness,' said the doctor, straightening up. 'For a first baby, this one is intent on arriving very quickly. We must get the Princess to hospital.'

'Then do it!' he said urgently.

It all became very blurred after that—the screeching of wheels and the flashing of lights, and the pain getting more and more intense. In the back of the ambulance Lucy's nails bit into Guido's palm.

'Don't leave me,' she gasped. 'Will you?'

He wanted to tell her that Royal husbands did not stay with their wives during labour, but he saw the stark terror in her eyes and sensed her isolation with a perception which he would have usually blunted.

'Of course I will stay,' he bit out. 'Don't worry, Lucy—it's going to be all right. Everything is going to be all right.'

But he was aware that his words were hollow—for who could utter them with any degree of certainty? Nature was in charge now—random and cruel nature—who could change lives at one capricious stroke. His mouth tightened and he smoothed a damp strand of hair back from Lucy's brow. He wasn't going to think about that now.

Lucy's preconceived ideas about how she'd wanted to have the baby, while floating in a tank of water, were immediately banished by the midwife, and soon she was on a hard bed with her legs in stirrups. She tried not to thrash around.

'Oh, what must you think of me, Guido?' she moaned.

He was having difficulty speaking. 'I think you're pretty damned wonderful, if you must know.'

Had the gas and air made her completely uninhibited? 'You'll never fancy me again now you've seen me like this!' she wailed.

This was more like the Lucy he knew! A wry smile curved his mouth as he saw the midwife's look of horror. 'Let us not concern ourselves with that right now, *cara*,' he murmured smoothly. But then he saw her face twist with pain once more, and an unfamiliar wave of helplessness washed over him.

'Can you not help her?' he demanded.

'We are doing everything we can, Highness!'

Lucy was in a hot, dark tunnel of torture. There were instructions not to push when she wanted to push, and then to push when she was so tired she could barely open her eyes. And the pain! She whimpered, and then drew in all her strength for one last, huge effort.

The midwife was encouraging her, and Guido was saying something disbelieving in Italian, and then their baby daughter was born—all black-haired, like her daddy, and covered in gunk.

They put her on Lucy's stomach, and she stared down at her with a kind of wonder.

'Hello,' she said tremulously, and a tear of relief began to slide from between her eyelids. She scrubbed it away with her fist before she looked over to see Guido's reaction.

But he had gone to the window and was standing

there, completely motionless, staring out at the fresh, pale light of the spring day.

'Guido?' she whispered tentatively.

He turned round, but his proud and beautiful face gave nothing away. As usual.

He bent to gently kiss her forehead, and then to brush his mouth against the cheek of his daughter.

It took a moment or two before he was able to speak with the composure which was expected of him.

'Well done, Lucy,' he said. 'She is very beautiful.' Then he turned to the midwife and the doctor with a formal smile. 'And may I thank you for all your hard work?'

Lucy sank back onto the pillows as they took her daughter away to clean her, and an overwhelming wave of sadness swelled up to hit her like a fist. She did not know what she had been expecting him to say, but it had not been enough.

Maybe she was chasing the impossible—for with Guido it was never enough.

CHAPTER THIRTEEN

THE books said that having any new baby was exhausting, but Lucy decided that it must be especially so if you had one as lively—and intelligent!—as Nicole Katerina Marguerite Cacciatore. The new Princess seemed to have an aversion to sleeping at times when babies should be sleeping. It was a good thing, thought Lucy, that she compensated for her active nature by being the most beautiful baby in the entire world. But then she would be, wouldn't she?

For she looked exactly like her father.

Guido glanced up one morning to find Lucy yawning, dark shadows having planted faint blue thumbprints beneath her eyes, and he frowned.

'*Cara*, this cannot go on.'

'What can't?' The fact that he hadn't come near her since the baby had been born, bar the odd brief, perfunctory hug? Or that he had gone back to being that restless and wary Guido, who walked around like a caged lion?

He seemed to have slipped away from her again, and she wondered if he would ever come back. A woman who had newly given birth didn't usually feel beguiling enough to play the temptress. Even in normal circumstances...

'You are exhausted,' he pointed out. Her tiredness

was almost palpable. He had taken to sleeping in an adjoining room, because the last thing she needed at a time like this was a husband who couldn't keep his hands off her. 'I have never seen anyone look so tired.'

'Well, new mothers generally are.'

'Then why not engage a nanny?' he questioned.

Lucy bit her lip and poured herself a cup of coffee. She could go on bottling up her fears for ever, but that meant that nothing would change and she would be destined to spend a life only half lived. Trying to be all things to a man who seemed content to operate on such a superficial level of existence that he didn't even want to share her bed now the baby had been born!

'Because I don't need a nanny,' she said stubbornly.

'Maybe you do. Look at you! A nanny would take over at night—at least let you get some proper sleep.'

'I want to do it all myself,' she emphasised. 'All my friends do.'

He wanted to point out that her friends were not princesses, except he suspected the argument would fall on deaf ears—for Lucy was weaving a strong bond with their baby which, as a father, he should commend. So what, exactly, was the problem? He drank a mouthful of inky coffee which was much too hot, but he didn't wince.

Sometimes he watched as she played with Nicole, thinking herself unobserved. From the shadows he saw the way she kissed the tiny baby head, listened to the crooning little sounds she made, and long-buried memories resurfaced. He remembered standing by the door while his mother cradled his new brother, experiencing a sense of being an outsider—which every older sibling must feel.

And then...

He drew a deep breath, pushing the pain to the back of his mind. Patience was not one of his virtues, but he was beginning to recognise that it was what new mothers needed more than anything else.

'Okay,' he agreed. 'But she could help you during the day. How about that?'

Lucy looked at him—casting him the bait and hoping that he would take it. 'But the baby gives me a *raison d'être*,' she said quietly. 'You've set up an office for yourself and you spend all day working in it. What else am I going to do if someone else is taking care of her?'

'Ella manages.'

But Ella had Nico, and they were a couple in the truest sense of the word. She drew a deep breath. 'Ella is settled.'

His eyes narrowed. 'And you're not?'

'Not really, no. How can I be? Everything feels so...so...*temporary*. You don't want to be here.'

'That is not true,' he said heavily.

'Guido, you know it is! If I said yes, you'd be out of this room booking tickets to New York this morning!'

'Then say yes,' he said softly.

She saw the appeal in his dark eyes. Was it pride

which was stopping her, or fear of the unknown? Didn't there have to be compromise for marriage to work? And if he wouldn't—then wasn't it down to her?

'If that's what you really want,' she said woodenly. 'Then I will.'

How plain she made her feelings for him! His voice was cold as he put his napkin down on the table and stood up. 'Oh, please, Lucy! Anyone would imagine that I was proposing rehousing you in some slum! There is no problem—we will stay here if that is what you prefer. That was, after all, the agreement.' He paused. 'My father would like you to take Nicole to visit him this morning.'

Lucy's eyes grew wider. The King had been very sick and unable to see his new granddaughter. His sons visited him daily, but he had been advised against all other callers.

'He's better?' she questioned hopefully.

'Well, he is better than before.' He shrugged. 'There is no magic cure—but it will bring him great joy to see his granddaughter.'

'You'll…you'll come with me?' Her voice was nervous. Her meetings with Mardivino's ruler had been infrequent. He had shown her nothing but kindness, but, despite his frailty, he was still a formidable man.

He shook his head. 'I have work to do.' He saw the hurt which clouded her eyes. 'And he wants to see you alone,' he finished softly.

She knew that it was pointless to ask him why. He

would shrug and give her that mocking look of his, tell her that she would find out soon enough, that it was not his place to tell her of his father's wishes—if indeed he knew them—or to second-guess them if he did not.

She took ages dressing Nicole in a pretty little Broderie Anglais dress—which she was promptly sick over. By the time she had changed her she had time only to throw on a floaty dress which she hoped disguised her post-pregnancy tummy. She brushed her hair until it shone, then shot a slightly despairing look at herself in the mirror. Hardly the image of the calm and composed Princess which no doubt the King would be expecting!

But for once Nicole behaved like a little angel—or maybe it was the quietness and calm of the King's apartments which quietened her, for she was fast asleep in Lucy's arms by the time they were summoned inside.

The King lay resting in a bed which had been turned to face the gardens outside, where the bright and beautiful flowers danced. He was very old now, but you could see that he had once been a strong and powerful man, and his face bore the hallmarks of pride and dignity. His faded eyes had once been black, like his sons', and for the first time Lucy realised that his mouth was very like Guido's.

She managed some sort of awful attempt at a curtsey, but he shook his head and patted the side of the bed.

'Sit,' he commanded.

As she sat, he leaned forward. An ever-present nurse sprang to attention but he waved her away.

'Leave us,' he commanded.

'But your Royal Highness—'

'Leave!'

The nurse left and the King examined Nicole's face carefully, then lifted his head and gave Lucy a tired smile.

'She is very beautiful,' he observed.

Lucy was trying to remember all the etiquette of not speaking until she was spoken to, but in the circumstances it was difficult—and when it all boiled down to it wasn't she just like any proud mother showing off her baby to his grandpop?

'Yes, she is, isn't she?' She beamed. 'She's got Guido's eyes, of course, and his colouring—'

'But your nose, I think,' he said unexpectedly.

'Well, yes,' answered Lucy, pleased. 'I think so.'

'And my late wife's name. Nicole.'

'Yes. Guido wanted it.'

'A medieval French name,' he observed rather dreamily. 'Although I believe it is popular again now.'

They sat for a few moments in companionable silence, watching and listening while Nicole nestled in Lucy's arms and made little sucking noises.

'Would you like to hold her?' she asked tentatively, but the King shook his head.

'My arms are too weak to cope with such vigorous life,' he said sadly, but then his faded eyes twinkled at her. 'And, if the truth were known, the Princes of

Mardivino were not raised to deal with infants! Nico has broken the mould of that, of course,' he observed thoughtfully.

'Yes.'

He looked at her properly then, and she could see the quiet gleam of perception in his dark eyes. 'And Guido? He is…what is that term they use for fathers nowadays?'

'Hands-on?'

He smiled. 'Yes. Is Guido…hands-on?'

Lucy chose her words carefully. 'Not really. He loves her, of course—but he's one of those men who's almost a bit too frightened to pick her up, in case he drops her.'

The King appeared to digest this. 'I should never have sent him to America,' he said suddenly.

It was such an astonishing thing for him to say that Lucy just stared at him. In the long silence which followed, the King seemed to be deciding whether or not to speak.

'When his mother died I think I went a little bit mad,' he admitted eventually, and then he gave a ragged little sigh. 'It was such a shock, you see.'

Lucy said nothing, for there was nothing in the etiquette books to prepare you for a disclosure like this one.

'Nico was just a baby, of course—and oblivious to what was going on.'

'But he would have missed his mother,' Lucy pointed out.

He nodded. 'Of course he did. And for a while he

was a lost little baby. But his physical needs were such that his nurse was able to fulfil them. Gianferro was different—he was almost eight, and my heir, and as such he had always been treated in isolation from the other two. His whole life has been a role of preparation,' he said. 'He has always been taught to adapt to the changes that time brings.'

Lucy thought that little had changed—that Gianferro still lived his life in isolation. She held the baby closer and carried on looking at the King. Some instinct told her that he was leading up to something, but she didn't know what it was.

'But Guido was shattered,' he said quietly. 'He was especially close to his mother. For a while it seemed that the Palace was in uproar. Indeed, the whole island was—my people grieved for her so—and when my wife's sister offered to take him for the summer in Connecticut—I…well, I seized the opportunity.'

'You did what you thought was best,' said Lucy staunchly. But people's thinking was often muddled when they were grieving. And no one could predict the effect that their actions would have on the future.

'How do you think he felt?' asked the King.

She didn't question him on why he had asked her, or begin to wonder whether he had heard rumours that she and Guido were not happy. The important thing was that he *had* asked, and she must answer. Truthfully.

'He must have felt very…alone,' she said slowly, and a wave of guilt rocked her. How blinkered she had been. She had been so busy thinking about what *she* wanted—about what was best for *her*—that she had never stopped to think about why Guido was the way he was, why he acted the way he did.

She tried to imagine his confusion and his anger and his hurt at the time. Close to the mother who had been so cruelly taken from him, and then sent away from the only home he knew. He must have felt as if he wasn't wanted. No wonder he found it difficult to adapt to life on Mardivino. And she had selfishly refused to understand why.

But he never talked about it—he never talked about anything close to him.

And can you really blame him?

He had been too young to articulate his feelings at the time—he must have just blocked them out to make them bearable. And perhaps the habit had become one which had followed him into adulthood, impossible to break.

The King was looking at her, but he made no comment on the way she had bitten her lip in sorrow and self-recrimination.

'He never cried, you know,' he said suddenly. 'Not once.'

Feeling that if she heard any more then her heart would break, Lucy stared down at Nicole. A fierce need to make things right filled her with a new kind of determination. She didn't need the fairytale love-story—for how many people ever got that?—but if she could make her daughter happy, then surely she could make Guido happy, too. But how? Well, she could start by agreeing to move to New York! That was no hardship, really, was it?

She stared at the King, seeing him begin to wilt a little, and as if summoned by an invisible command the nurse reappeared. Lucy got to her feet. 'Thank you for seeing me today, your Serene Highness,' she said quietly.

'It has been my pleasure.' He pointed to his forehead, and, immensely moved, she bent to kiss it, then held the baby forward for him to do the same to her.

She was about to move away when his next words halted her.

'Do you ever sing to her?' he asked.

Lucy blinked. 'Occasionally. Why?'

'There is a lullaby, a French lullaby—''*Bonne Nuit Cher Enfant*''—do you know it?'

Lucy shook her head.

'Then learn it, and sing it to her some time.' He smiled conspiratorially. 'Our little secret.'

Their eyes met and Lucy realised that he did not have long to live. For why else would have said such an extraordinary thing? Abandoning Court formality to suggest she learnt a lullaby!

But she had learned so much else during her unconventional conversation with the King, and she was lost in thought as she made her way back from his apartments.

When she arrived in her own suite of rooms it was to find a message from Guido, telling her that he had unexpectedly had to go to the other side of the island, and he would be back the following day.

Her heart sank. She had been bursting to tell him her news, and now he wasn't around to hear it! And it wasn't the kind of thing that she wanted to tell him over the phone...she wanted to see his face.

Well, she had waited this long to come to her senses. A little longer wouldn't hurt her.

After lunch, she took Nicole for a walk, and happened to see Nico in the Palace gardens. He was wearing shorts and a singlet and was dripping with sweat. He had obviously been out running. Lucy smiled. It was times like this that really emphasised the fact that this was a family home as well as a Palace.

Well, maybe not for her. Not any more.

Yet, strangely enough, the idea now gave her no disquiet. She could live here for as long as she wanted to—but what was the point if Guido was unhappy? Inevitably, he would do what he had done once before—start taking more and more frequent trips to New York. Only with a baby she would not find it so easy to follow him...

'Hello, Nico,' she said.

'Hi!' he panted, and stopped to peer into the pram. 'How is she?'

'Gorgeous.' She looked at him. 'Nico?'

'Mmm?' His dark eyes crinkled at the corners.

'Do you know a lullaby called *"Bonne Nuit..."* something?'

'*"Bonne Nuit Cher Enfant"*?'

'That's the one!'

'Yeah, I know it.' He raised his eyebrows. 'Why?'

'Well, I wondered if you...' This was very important—she didn't know how, or why—she just knew that it was. 'Nico, will you teach it to me?'

CHAPTER FOURTEEN

DUSK was falling on the Palace by the time Guido returned, and he stretched and yawned as he walked along the long marble corridor leading to their apartments.

It had been years since he had visited the western side of the island, and he had been impressed to see the result of his brother's hard work. Nico was slowly helping to build up the infrastructure on Mardivino—to improve the roads and access to more remote parts of the island—but without destroying any of the natural and stunningly beautiful habitat. Indeed, the small fishing village of Lejana was as picturesque as any place he had visited. But maybe he had been viewing it with new eyes...

For Guido had found himself appreciating the landscape in a way that he had always seemed too busy to do before. That thing about making the most of the little things—taking time to stand and stare. Maybe having Nicole had changed him more than he'd realised. His heart gave a little leap at the thought that he would soon see her again. He glanced at his watch. If Lucy hadn't already put her to bed.

Briefly, his eyes closed as he thought of Lucy, and the longing and frustration gnawed away at him. Sometimes discoveries took an awful long time to make, and he knew now that he had not been fair to her—in so many ways.

Quietly, he opened the door to their suite, and then a sound stopped him in his tracks. He froze as he heard a voice singing a tune so familiar that it twisted his heart around.

Lucy's voice.

The words wafted through the still, early-evening air.

'Bonne nuit cher enfant...'

Guido closed his eyes.

'Quand tu dors dans mes bras...'

He stood motionless as a statue until the final lilting strains.

'Comme un ange dans mes bras.'

He did not feel the tears which lay damp on his face. He moved like a man in a dream—maybe he was—until he opened the door to the nursery and saw them. Mother with child. Rocking gently in the big old chair which had seen generations of Royal babies nursed.

And there it was—his past, his present and his future, all merged into the tableau silhouetted by the window.

Lucy looked up and her lips parted in disbelief. 'Guido?' she whispered, as if she had seen a ghost— and maybe she had—for this was her husband as she had never seen him before.

'I didn't know you knew that song,' he said unsteadily.

'Do you?' It was one of those unnecessary questions, but it needed to be asked. It was a floodgate question.

He nodded. 'Of course I do. My mother used to sing it.'

So! With swift care she deposited Nicole in her crib and went to him, brushing away his tears with gentle fingertips. Then she wrapped her arms tightly around him with not a thought other than to comfort him, not caring if he wanted this from her or not—because right then he *needed* it. They sometimes said that it took a weak man to cry, but Lucy knew that was wrong.

For strong men could cry, too.

'Oh, my darling,' she said softly. 'My darling, darling Guido—what is wrong? Tell me.'

But a lifetime of not talking about things didn't just vanish in an instant, and Lucy knew that she had to help him—show him the way forward—let him know that a life lived to the full in *all* the ways that mattered was a better life for them all.

She drew a deep breath for courage, praying that in his pain he wouldn't push her away. 'You never grieved for your mother,' she said slowly, and saw him flinch. 'You never even cried. Your father sent you away and you felt you weren't wanted any more. You were a lost soul in America, and when you came back it didn't feel like home. Nowhere did, nor ever has.'

'Who told you this?'

'Your father gave me the bare outline—the rest of it I filled in myself. Some of it I had already guessed.

That's why he told me to learn the lullaby and sing it to Nicole—'

'My father told you to do *that*?' he demanded incredulously.

Lucy nodded. 'He must have known that sooner or later you would hear me singing it.'

He was dazed, like a man who had been knocked out and was slowly coming round again. 'That is a remarkably perceptive thing for him to have done,' he said, still on a disbelieving note.

'I think he *is* a perceptive man,' she said. 'But as King he rarely shows it quite so openly. Or maybe his position doesn't allow him to.' And then she realised that perhaps there were other reasons why the King had enlightened her. That she had her own part to play in the healing process.

'Don't be hard on him for what happened, Guido,' she said softly. 'He acted with the best possible motives. He was missing your mother and having to help the people of Mardivino to adjust. Maybe he knew that there was no time to give to a five-year-old boy who was grieving. But he loves you,' she finished. 'He loves you very much.'

She prayed again, for the courage and the strength to say what she knew she had to without prejudice. Not because she wanted anything back from him— well, she did—but because Guido needed to hear this.

'As I do,' she said softly, and she looked up at him, her voice and her eyes very clear and very steady. 'As I do.'

Guido heard the deep love in her voice, unvarnished by any kind of vanity, and he gave a small cry, as if he had been wounded. A sweet, answering emotion began to lick warmth into his cold heart. He tightened his arms to enfold her closer and thought what a fool he had been. He buried his face in the sweet nectar of her hair, and for the first time in his life allowed his feelings to wash over him.

They bathed him with a bitter pain and regret until he thought he could bear it no longer, and then, inexorably, the tide turned and they gave way to a blessed kind of peace and hope. He raised his head and looked down at her.

'Will you forgive me, *cara*?' he said shakily.

'Why?' Her eyes widened. 'What have you done?'

Now he could read her own fears. *Dio*, but he had never stopped to think about how she might really be feeling herself, deep down. Was that because he had not cared? Or had not dared?

He touched her lips with his own. 'Not enough,' he said gently. 'Not nearly enough.'

'Guido, you're talking in riddles.'

'Then that does not bode well for the future, *cara mia*,' he responded. 'Since I have just come to my senses!'

'Guido! Please! What is it?'

'I want you to listen to me now, and hear me out. Do you think you can do that?'

She closed her eyes, praying that he hadn't decided he couldn't go on…not before she had had a chance to tell him that she was prepared to change. If he didn't want love then she would deal with it—because she wanted to work at her marriage. To do anything in her power to make it better. Weren't some Royal marriages based on that kind of understanding anyway? All she knew was that she didn't want to lose him.

'I have been a selfish, stupid fool, Lucy,' he said bitterly. 'I have just taken and taken—without even considering what it is that you might want. Without bothering to give anything back.'

'Guido, I—'

'Weren't you going to hear me out?' he queried gravely.

She nodded, because now she doubted whether any words would come, for her throat was knotted by the terror which was beating hotly through her veins.

'It was insensitive and thoughtless of me to expect you to live in New York.'

She wanted to say *But*… Except that she had promised to listen…

'Yesterday I went to visit Lejana—do you know where it is?'

'Isn't it on the coast by the Western Isles?'

A smile of satisfaction curved his lips. 'You know your Mardivinian geography,' he approved.

'Well, our daughter will need to—it's her heritage!' she retorted, and his smile grew wider. 'What about it?'

'There is a big plot there that we could build a house on.' He saw her frown. 'But if you want to stay in Solajoya, then you can—any damned part you choose!' He then made what was, for him, the ultimate sacrifice. 'We can even carry on living at the Palace if that's what you want.'

'But I don't!'

He narrowed his eyes. 'Don't what?'

'I don't want to live on Mardivino—I want to live in New York!'

Now he was confused. 'You do?'

'Yes!'

He frowned. 'So what's changed your mind?'

'I want to make our marriage work, Guido. You won't be happy living here, and if you're not happy then I won't be either—and everyone knows that women are much better at adapting than men.' She drew a badly needed breath. 'So I will.'

He began to laugh, and once he had started he couldn't stop—but then he had never laughed with quite such uninhibited joy before. It was like balm to his soul, music to an ear starved of sound.

Lucy stared at him as if he had taken leave of his senses. 'Shh! You'll wake Nicci!'

He pressed his lips together like a schoolboy trying not to giggle in church. 'Let's get this straight, Lucy. You want to live in New York because I do—and I want to live on Mardivino because *you* do?'

'Um…well, yes, I suppose so. Oh, Guido—this is terrible—it's like Catch 22! What are we going to do?'

'I don't think we need to decide *right* this minute, do you? I think that there are rather more important things to do.' Like finding the right words to convince her that he didn't care where the hell he was, just as long as she would be by his side. He felt like a blind man who had just stumbled into the light. And that, he knew, was the restorative power of love.

'Guido...'

'Shh.' He raised her hand to his lips and kissed it, then wrapped his palm around it very firmly and led her over to the crib. In silence they stood there, looking down on their daughter. Her dark lashes were like crescent moons on her perfect skin, and her little rosebud of a mouth pursed itself and made tiny sucking noises. One miniature arm was raised above her head, and it ended in a tiny clenched fist.

'Do you think she'll be a fighter?' he whispered.

And Lucy recognised that she had so nearly thrown in the towel and given up on Guido.

'Oh, I hope so,' she answered fervently. 'I really hope so.'

EPILOGUE

IT WASN'T all plain sailing from there on in—of course it wasn't. No marriage ever was, and especially not one which had started out like Lucy and Guido's. Guido had much to learn, and so did Lucy—about living together, about being newly-weds and new parents—oh, the list went on and on!

Mainly they had to learn about each other, but the magical thing was that they both wanted to—with a passion which made the steep learning curve seem like a doddle, and all the little hiccups fade into insignificance.

What had started as a tiny thaw in the ice which surrounded Guido's heart melted under the onslaught of the love given to him by his wife and his daughter. It was crazy, but love really *did* change everything—the way he felt, the way he viewed the world, and his place in it.

His own love flourished, and he learned that to show it did not make him less of a man, but more—for it made him a complete man. And as Guido's love grew, so Lucy basked in it, growing more secure and more confident—certainly enough for the feisty streak in her nature to re-emerge.

The two of them were back to their magnificent combative best! In fact, as Gianferro remarked rather drily to Guido, it was something of a relief for the rest of the family now the house he'd had built for them in Lejana was finished!

It was, Lucy decided, the most beautiful house she had ever seen. So airy and light and full of windows—all the better to see the commanding sapphire of the nearby sea, which beat and roared and filled the air with its siren music.

The grounds sloped down to their own private beach—where Nicole would learn to swim and sail, taught by her father, who these days had the time.

Because Lucy had been right all along, Guido realised. She had told him often enough that he was achieving for the sake of achievement's sake, and he didn't need to do it any more. If he wasn't careful then life would pass him by while he was tying up unnecessary deals. And now that he had a family of his own the lure of making money in his property business had begun to pale—especially if you looked at it with the cool logic he always liked to employ—except maybe where his wife was concerned.

Even if you discounted his inherited wealth—which he had put into a Trust Fund for Nicole and any future children—he had earned all the money he could want, and more.

So he'd stopped wheeling and dealing across the globe, and put his energies into Mardivino instead—and his expertise in property stood him in good stead to advise on issues of architecture and planning.

As a couple, they stayed away from a lot of Royal functions—unless, as Lucy joked, they needed to 'swell the numbers'. They were happy to help out when needed, but that was all. Guido hated the rigidity of Court life, and Lucy wanted to create for him as normal and as happy a nuclear family as she could. The kind he had grown up missing...

The two of them were sitting on their terrace one evening, watching the setting sun sink like a blazing lollipop into the vast sea. It was the end of a baking hot summer day—there had been a family picnic, and the last of their guests had gone. Nico and Ella and Leo had been there—Ella pregnant with their second child, being fussed over by her husband, while their son played happily on the sand with Nicole, watched by an ever-attentive nanny.

Gianferro had—surprisingly—agreed to make a place in his busy schedule to come, too. As the King's health declined, so Gianferro's workload increased. Lucy had thought how utterly exhausted he looked as she watched him build a sandcastle for Leo to demolish, and how rare it was to see him let his guard down.

Bathed in the red-gold light of the setting sun, Lucy turned to her husband, revelling in the fact that his lean, hard body could look so relaxed these days. When she had first known him he had been so fired-up—always restless—as if he had been constantly seeking something but hadn't quite known what it was. Had he found it?

'Didn't you think Gianferro looked tired today?' she questioned slowly.

Guido shrugged. 'No more than usual.'

'Well, I think he drives himself too hard.'

'But that, *cara mia*, is the natural consequence of his destiny.'

'Can't you and Nico help him a bit more?'

He surveyed her with a small sigh of satisfaction— for her heart was deep and generous. With each day that passed his regard for her as a woman increased, and sometimes he wondered what he had ever done to deserve such a woman as this.

'No, my love,' he answered simply. 'We cannot. For one day Gianferro will be King, and Kings must always reign alone.'

Lucy's heart melted. 'How lonely it must be.'

'Inevitably.'

'And he doesn't even have a wife—nor any sign of one!'

Guido's eyes narrowed. 'That, of course, is an entirely different concern—and one which it is within his power to change. For he needs to have children if he wants to continue his bloodline. If not, then our own children stand in line to rule Mardivino one day.'

Lucy had known this on some unacknowledged level, but hearing Guido say it made the prospect seem frighteningly real. Her eyes widened. 'You don't want that for them, do you?'

He tried to imagine his little Nicole as Queen and his mouth tightened. It was hard to think of any child of his having to endure the trappings and tribulations of Majesty, but he forced himself to let his misgivings go, as Lucy had taught him. For what was the point of worrying about something which might never happen?

'No, I do not,' he said softly. 'But I cannot fight what might come to pass—I must embrace it whole-heartedly. We will wait and see what transpires.'

'Perhaps we ought to try and find a wife for Gianferro!'

He raised his dark eyebrows by a fraction as he pictured quite clearly his eldest brother's reaction to such an attempt at matchmaking. He would be out-raged! 'Or perhaps not,' he said drily.

Lucy bit her lip. 'Do you think…do you think he'll ever marry for love?'

'Ahh…' He held his hand out to her and Lucy took it, going to sit on his knee, her hands holding on to his broad, strong shoulders as if he were her anchor in a choppy sea. He shook his head. 'No, I do not— he is not in a position to allow himself such a luxury.'

She affected indignation. 'So you think that love is a luxury, do you?'

He smiled. 'No, my darling,' he said softly, and lifted his fingertips to touch the silken surface of her cheek. 'I think it is a necessity.'

She saw the sudden fierceness of his expression, heard the intensity behind his words, and she waited, a little flicker of hope burning away in her heart as she looked at him expectantly. For while Guido had learned to show his love in every way that counted he was still slow to speak it. It was as though—even for a man who could already speak four fluently—the language of love was the hardest of all!

'You are my world, Lucy,' he said simply, and he could see her beautiful mouth begin to wobble. That fleeting trace of insecurity both wounded him and spurred him on to tell her how much she meant to him. How very much. 'As vital to me as the water I drink and the air that I breathe. You are the sun that rises in the morning and the moon that lights my evening sky.' There was a pause, heavy with emotion, as he lifted her chin and dazzled her with the ebony fire from his eyes. 'I love you, *cara* Lucy. And I lay down my life for you.'

'Oh…oh, Guido…Guido.' She was not aware that a tear had begun to trickle its way down her cheek—not until he gave a soft smile and traced its path with the tip of his finger, then solemnly lifted the finger to his mouth to suck the salt away.

'No tears,' he said. 'No tears. Why are you crying when I have just told you how much I love you?'

She nodded, gulping them back. 'Because… because that's the most wonderful thing anyone has ever said to me!'

'I should think so, too!' he said fervently. 'For I am your husband!'

'Yes.' Her husband. Her lover. Her friend. Father to her child and—oh, so much more than that. For he was her sun, too—and her moon and her stars. As vital and vibrant as the mighty sea which filled their house with such incomparable light. 'I love you so much, Guido,' she said shakily.

He took her into his arms and began to stroke her until she relaxed, as molten and as malleable as soft wax, and at some point the stroking stopped and the kissing began. Deep, searching kisses—silent declarations of feelings which were bigger than both of them.

And some time after that he pulled her down onto the wooden decking of the moonwashed terrace. He slipped off the bikini she wore, and slid off his shorts—and when he entered her it felt like the most elemental thing which had ever happened to her. And the most precious. As if all those acts of fulfilling love had merely been a rehearsal for this, the real thing.

There was just the sound of lips exploring and small sighs of wonder as their bodies moved in harmony—like the planets which danced in the heavens around them—until at last their cries of mutual pleasure rang out and were lost in the music of the waves.

'I love you, Lucy,' he murmured against her lips.

'I love you, too,' she murmured back.

He kissed her hair and yawned, and began to wriggle into sleep, and Lucy rested her face against the muffled pounding of his heart and sighed with pure happiness as his naked body enfolded hers.

It was a very good thing, she decided, just before her eyes closed, that theirs was such a *private* house…

If you enjoyed what you just read,
then we've got an offer you can't resist!

Take 2 bestselling love stories FREE!

Plus get a FREE surprise gift!

Clip this page and mail it to Harlequin Reader Service®

IN U.S.A.	IN CANADA
3010 Walden Ave.	P.O. Box 609
P.O. Box 1867	Fort Erie, Ontario
Buffalo, N.Y. 14240-1867	L2A 5X3

YES! Please send me 2 free Harlequin Presents® novels and my free surprise gift. After receiving them, if I don't wish to receive anymore, I can return the shipping statement marked cancel. If I don't cancel, I will receive 6 brand-new novels every month, before they're available in stores! In the U.S.A., bill me at the bargain price of $3.80 plus 25¢ shipping & handling per book and applicable sales tax, if any*. In Canada, bill me at the bargain price of $4.47 plus 25¢ shipping & handling per book and applicable taxes**. That's the complete price and a savings of at least 10% off the cover prices—what a great deal! I understand that accepting the 2 free books and gift places me under no obligation ever to buy any books. I can always return a shipment and cancel at any time. Even if I never buy another book from Harlequin, the 2 free books and gift are mine to keep forever.

106 HDN DZ7Y
306 HDN DZ7Z

Name	(PLEASE PRINT)	
Address	Apt.#	
City	State/Prov.	Zip/Postal Code

Not valid to current Harlequin Presents® subscribers.

Want to try two free books from another series?
Call 1-800-873-8635 or visit www.morefreebooks.com.

* Terms and prices subject to change without notice. Sales tax applicable in N.Y.
** Canadian residents will be charged applicable provincial taxes and GST.
 All orders subject to approval. Offer limited to one per household.
 ® are registered trademarks owned and used by the trademark owner and or its licensee.

PRES04R   ©2004 Harlequin Enterprises Limited

Introducing a brand-new trilogy by

Sharon Kendrick

**Passion, power and privilege—the dynasty
continues with these handsome princes…**

Welcome to Mardivino—a beautiful and
wealthy Mediterranean island principality,
with a prestigious and glamorous royal family.
There are three Cacciatore princes—Nicolo,
Guido and the eldest, the heir, Gianferro.

**This month (May 2005) you can meet Nico in
THE MEDITERRANEAN
PRINCE'S PASSION #2466**

**Next month (June 2005) read Guido's story in
THE PRINCE'S LOVE-CHILD #2472**

**Coming in July: Gianferro's story in
THE FUTURE KING'S BRIDE #2478**

Seduction and Passion Guaranteed!